Chateau GISELLE
Mis en Bouteille au Chateau
CHATEAU
GISELLE
Merlot
1984
Lapis
VINEYARD
PROSSER
WA

FOR THE SAKE

OF THE VINE
Adria Lang

A Tigress Publishing Book
Copyright 2009 Tigress Publishing

ISBN: 978-1-59404-024-5
1-59404-024-9

Library of Congress Control Number: 2009923852
Printed in the United States of America

Based on original concept by: D. Michael Tomkins
Original Art, Interior & Cover Design: Steve Montiglio
Editor: Amelia Boldaji

10 9 8 7 6 5 4 3 2 1

Tigress Publishing
4837 Fauntleroy Way SW # 103
Seattle, Washington 98116

BASED ON AN ORIGINAL

CONCEPT BY

D. MICHAEL

TOMKINS

Original ART

AND DESIGN

STEVE

MONTIGLIO

PROLOGUE

·CLAY·

"Pick one."

Zachary looked up at his father. The low autumn sun was hitting Horst Bartlett's profile at just the right angle, making him look as large and grand as an ancient unnamed God. In front of him, in his vine-weathered hands, the winemaker presented a cluster of grapes. Horst's wry smile suggested to the boy some kind of game, which, if played correctly, would result in such sublime joy that one or both of them might burst into flames.

Zachary glanced around the vineyard for his twin sister Angelina. He was that kind of child—sharing came naturally. He spotted her in a cloud of dust, chasing a few of the migrant workers' children through the vines.

"What about Angie?"

"That monkey can play later. Go on."

Horst bent down on his right knee. The telltale dirt patch on every pair of light linen pants he owned was as much a part of his person as his Berliner forehead.

Zachary wondered, perhaps not consciously till many years later, how his father was able to spend all day in the vineyards and come out looking as pristine as when he went in save for that lone dirt patch on his right pant leg. It was as if the vines parted for him, ever so slightly, out of respect for their master—the all knowing, all seeing creator that nurtured them from shoot to bottle. The attentive, never arbitrary, yet ultimately cruel, *Master of the Vines*.

Zachary scrunched up his face. They had been on

the hill picking grapes all day. What made this cluster special? Still, he chose carefully. A shiny one caught his eye. It looked like a black marble compared to its neighbors, which for some reason lacked its radiance. He was confident in his choice.

"This one," Zachary said proudly.

"That one, eh? Let me see it."

Zachary handed the grape to his father who held it gently between two fingers, examining it in the sunlight as if it were a rare gem.

"She's a good one, Zachary. A beauty. Here, hold her for a moment." Horst's Franco-Germanic accent was perfect for communicating with children. It was soft and lilting like the man himself, or at least the man he was in those days.

Zachary put out his hands, palms up, and received the little grape messiah tenderly. It rolled there, a perfect sphere with its puckered mouth flashing lewdly. Its underside was still a yeasty midnight azure, making the tiny miracle of nature look like a half moon, or a velvet acorn.

"What do you see?"

"A grape."

"What else?"

Zachary stared at his hands.

"Do you see the skin? Do you see how fragile it is?"

Zachary was entranced. "Uh-huh."

"If I were to run a blade over its skin and your skin, with the same pressure, I could break both."

With a dirty nail Horst traced an invisible line across his son's pudgy forearm.

"What about Angie's skin?"

"Angelina's too. And mine, and your mother's. We are all as fragile as this little grape. We start as a tiny shoot, then we grow into a vine, and eventually if the conditions are just right, we get to make something spectacular."

"Grapes?"

"First grapes, yes. Then wine. Wine!" Horst roared. As though to punctuate his little lesson with a somewhat cruel visual aid, Horst clapped his son's palms together flattening the little grapelet between them.

Zachary let the remaining dark skin fall from between his hands and wiped its juices on his overalls, consumed in a fit of sadistic giggles. Horst smiled and stood up, a thin sheath of sweat glistening on his brow. He was Dionysus during harvest season and everyone reveled in his spiritual intoxication.

Those days were the crowning jewels of Zach's childhood memories: long warm days, cool nights, getting lost in row after row of vines, the smell of the earth and sometimes even the river coming over the hills. It was a commune with nature so intimate it had all of them locked in a kind of anthropomorphic romance.

"Daddy? Do the vines miss the grapes when they get picked?"

"What?" Horst turned to his son suddenly and curiously. So much so that Zachary thought he had said something monumentally stupid.

"Nothing."

"No son, it's all right. You want to know if the vines miss the grapes?"

"I dunno."

Horst bent down on his knee again, this time on his left. To Zachary that had always seemed strange. He had no way of knowing that his father was so distracted by his question that it caused Horst to momentarily break from the part of his brain responsible for involuntary habits. That simple question filled Horst with more pure, unadulterated, parental pride then he had ever felt before or since. Later that night he would write in one of his notebooks:

HE IS TRULY MY BOY AND MY BOY IS AN AMAZEMENT. HE KNOWS BY SIMPLE INSTINCT WHAT IT TOOK ME MY WHOLE LIFE TO UNDERSTAND. THAT THE LIFE OF THE GRAPE DOES NOT CEASE WHEN IT IS SEVERED FROM THE VINE, BUT TRANSCENDS MUCH LIKE A HUMAN SOUL, THROUGH THE CRUDE AND PAINSTAKING PROCESSES OF FERMENTATION, AGING, BLENDING, FILTRATIONS, EG; PURGATORY —SPIRITUAL, EMBALMING—PHYSICAL. THE SOUL'S JOURNEY IS ONLY SUSPENDED, NOT STIFLED IT IS UP TO THE WINEMAKER TO RESURRECT IT THROUGH CAREFUL CHEMISTRY INVOLVING, BUT NOT LIMITED TO PRESSURE, TIME, TEMPERATURE, SACRIFICE, SWEAT, PAIN, OBSESSION, BLOOD, WITCHCRAFT, AND ALL-CONSUMING LOVE.

But those were afterthoughts, afterthoughts that gave birth to preliminary thoughts of another, darker, nature. When Horst looked at his five-year-old son and saw for the first time Zachary's face as a tiny mirror reflecting his own swelling pride, he spoke in a way that a child could grasp but never fully understand.

Zachary would not forget his father's words that day, as they marked both the apex of Horst's sanity and the beginnings of his madness.

"They don't miss them," he whispered, "they envy them."

She was a bartender. They were all bartenders lately but Zach was still one or two martini shakers away from picking up on his own embarrassing pattern. Angie would have noticed it ages ago but he tended to keep that part of his life, the picking up on *the ladies* part, on strict lock down around her. He didn't want to have to deal with his sister's scrutiny, her sarcastic comments, or her volatile nature in matters that should be his alone. They weren't kids anymore.

That being said, he still felt the need to sneak around or at least to do his dirty business in bars that Angie wouldn't think of frequenting. He had set out on many nights like this in the past. Covert, on foot, or maybe in a taxi, to any number of cornucopia sporting, hot toddy serving, cozy fire burning, cafés, bars or taverns to mingle with the drunken locals and the wide-eyed tourists. It was a torturous exercise in quaintness but he endured it for the greater good.

This particular bartender was a townie. She had no affiliation with Bard College whatsoever save calling the occasional drunken co-ed a cab at the end of the night after he or she had evacuated the contents of his or her stomach all over the carpeted floor of The Rhinebeck Tavern. And she was older than him. Probably ten years older, maybe more. The forest of age between them would start clearing as soon as his wine-goggles wore off.

Her name was Misty or maybe Missy, short for

Melissa? Who knew? They had bonded over a bottle of Kestrel's 6th Edition Lady in Red. And, Oh, wasn't that funny, Misty/Missy was *wearing* red. And in a certain light she kind of looked like the pin-up girl on the bottle, only a blonde. What an amazing coincidence! Zach was in a jovial mood after noticing it on the wine list. Kestrel Vintners sat beside Lapis, his family's winery, so in a way seeing that familiar label was almost like going home. Without actually having to get on a plane to deal with the psychos who raised him, of course.

He had offered her a glass and they exchanged their critique, hers probably some bullshit fragments of a wine tasting seminar her job forced her to attend, his pure genetic instinct.

She said Meritage, he said Blend.

"Oh, yeah…right. I always confuse the two."

She smelled red currants, he nosed sweet red pepper.

"Is that what that is? Cool."

She tasted vanilla and swallowed. He felt the rocky silt of his childhood cut him to the back of his palate and spat.

"Wow. You really are an expert."

"It's a lovely table wine."

She probably would have dropped her panties then and there had he not shown his age and mentioned that he kinda also played in a band. She politely asked to hear some of his songs, and gave him a split of overpriced Medoc to have while he waited for her to count her tips. An hour later they were at his house sucking face on a ratty sofa listening to *The Rotten Vines'* first and only recorded album.

Angie's vocals cut mercilessly through Zach's wine-induced haze and he vaguely recalled taking off a shoe and hurling it at the stereo, missing, and hitting his roommate Bob's framed *Big Lebowski* poster instead. It was a good excuse as any to crawl out from beneath Misty/Missy for a breather. He was hoping Bob would come home and tear him a new one, thus giving him an out, but such divine intervention was not to come, at least not that easily.

Misty—he was almost positive it was Misty—was indeed pushing forty, of this Zach was sure. Not that she had been raked across the coals or anything, but she had a look about her. It was a corrupting look that made him feel anxious and he nearly jumped out of his skin when she got up to use the bathroom. She suddenly seemed like the kind of woman who would handcuff him to a bed in a seedy hotel room and leave him there to be eaten by rats.

He smoked some pot. He looked at his video game system. Mario Super Sluggers was calling to him so he turned it on and pulled out his private stash of mall candy. He could hear Angie laughing at him in his mind's ear. Screw her.

After what seemed like an eternity, Misty emerged from the commode. He could feel her watching him but continued playing in hopes that she would get bored and make an excuse to leave. Instead, she sat beside him on the floor and helped herself to a buttered popcorn flavored jellybean.

"What up, Misty?"

"It's Karen. My son has this game."

Zach looked at her, sober.

"No shit?"

"I wipe the floor with him. How about I play you, and if I win you have to do exactly as I say?"

"And if I win?"

"I'll leave."

It wasn't a very long game. What Karen lacked in wine knowledge she made up for by being a goddamn Super Mario phenomenon. In return for winning she wanted to give him a Judo lesson. Of course they had to do it on a soft, bed-like surface. Zach was just beginning to enjoy the feeling of having her legs wrapped around the back of his neck when the phone rang. Zach ignored it, letting it go to voicemail three times before Karen eventually released her vice grip and demanded he pick it up.

"It might be an emergency," the mother in her said.

"How old is that son of yours anyway?"

"Eight…," she laughed and threw him his boxers, "…teen!"

"Jesus Christ…hello?—Is this a joke?—Who is this?—The Cayman Islands?"

"I get those fucking time-share calls all the time. Tell them to shove it up their asses." Karen was stretching out her hamstrings for round two.

"One minute. Okay. Okay."

"Just hang up. You got any more wine?"

Zach had gone white as a ghost when he turned around to face her. He lowered the phone into his lap slowly.

"Hey, honey? Are you okay?"

"I need to call my sister. I think our father just died."

The Bartlett twins, Zachary and Angelina, had bid farewell to Prosser, Washington five-and-a-half years earlier in pursuit of two things: higher education, and getting the hell out of Prosser, Washington. They chose Bard College for its location. Not to say that they didn't think highly of its fantastic liberal arts program, but priorities are priorities, and distance cast an imposing shadow over all others.

The school resides in New York's Hudson Valley, known for the likes of Teddy Roosevelt and Ichabod Crane, as well as numerous live action historical reenactment societies, a whole slew of aviation museums, Woodstock, the Catskills, fall foliage and all the trappings thereof, and, of course, its fondness of the grape.

That final and seemingly unrelated fact had set

their father's mind at rest just as the twins thought it might. Winemakers are trustworthy, dedicated, hardworking people. So if there were vineyards around Bard, how could it not be safe? In that respect Horst was like an Arizona Mormon sending his children to school in Salt Lake City. He knew they would be taken in and protected by the fold, in his case, of the grape leaf. As long as no one bothered to remind Horst that Bard College was a mere hour's drive from the evils of New York City, he was satisfied with their choice.

Tilda could give less than a crap. Their father's second wife—nickname: The Baroness—was a self-obsessed, money hoarding, shrew who was more concerned with Fendi bags and Prada shoes then anything that had to do with the twins. In their eyes Tilda had no problem watching them go. Once, in what they considered her failed attempt to get them to leave the country, Tilda suggested that they apply to schools in France, maybe somewhere near *Bordeaux*—hint-hint. And they would have too, Angie was obsessed with France in her teens, but causing The Baroness any amount of unnecessary pleasure was just too painful a thought to bear.

They also chose Bard because they both got in—the concept of separation was never once entertained—and off they went, a pair of matching, flaxen haired innocents, to the wild wiles of the east.

It didn't take them long to find their footing. By the end of the first year Angie had dyed her blonde hair blue-black and shaved the sides into what is commonly known as a faux-hawk. She got a pair of stilettos from Goodwill and wore them everywhere. Slips became dresses and she traded in half her wardrobe for a biker jacket that smelled eternally of cat piss.

Zach gained thirty pounds, joined the swim team, lost

fifteen, and rounded out at a nice 170 despite his persisting candy fetish. Once a girl told him he looked like a young James Bond, after which he bought a pair of tortoiseshell sunglasses and a vintage suit that came with pockets full of blind confidence and started getting himself laid.

The twins were cool so they did the obvious thing and started a band. Talent notwithstanding, *The Rotten Vines* turned out to be the gift that kept on giving. Apparently a geeky wine joke in Prosser played just as well in the Hudson Valley, and they found themselves getting loads of gigs based on their name alone. But it was when the movie *Sideways* came out that *The Rotten Vines* really took off. They started a following of kids who drank only Merlot because, like they preached at their shows, *"Bullshit Hollywood don't know fuck all about vino!"*

It made the local wineries happy since the film had all but dried up tourist demand for the unfairly scapegoated grape. It also made the twins, who were nineteen at the time, local celebrities.

In another more rebellious incarnation known as sophomore year, Angie gave up on wine. She started drinking straight vodka, speaking with a German accent, and telling people she and Zach were married—a move that didn't exactly thrill Zach but one he was powerless to do anything about. And he did see Angie as his ball and chain, if he imagined the chain as an umbilical cord and the ball as a large fraternal duplicate with skinny legs and a mohawk.

She started skipping classes to scout for gigs in New York City. They played their first city show at a famous Third Avenue dive bar called The Continental to a crowd consisting of ten members of the Hudson Valley Wine Club. The outing was listed on the Club's newsletter and offered as part of a package deal that included a day trip to FAO Schwartz and the Rockefeller Center Christmas tree.

The trouble started when a Tivoil local wearing an embroidered reindeer sweater asked to see the wine list. The bartender brought out a dusty jug of the only wine the bar served. It was a cheap magnum that had probably been open for months and tasted like balsamic vinegar. The scene got ugly when the Wine Club sent back not only the first round, but the second and third as well. When the manager found out they were all there to see *The Rotten Vines*, he had the band bumped off the set list and threw the lot of them out.

"Fuck it all," said Angie, "New York's for cavemen."

And that was that. By the end of junior year she was smoking cloves and listening to Shostakovich. Zach was over it too so he bought a video game system and started burning on a regular basis. In protest, Angie taught all their material (about five and a half songs) to a lesbian freshman and her boi-friend in a stunt she referred to as, "*Pulling a Dread Pirate Roberts.*" *The Rotten Vines*, in some mutant incarnation, continued to haunt the bars of Hudson Valley even in the twins' absence.

In their senior year the twins got separate apartments and six weeks into some long overdue individuality training, Zachary Bartlett got a call that interrupted far more than his first ever Judo lesson.

Zach looked at the clock and pulled on his jeans. Two forty-five in the morning. Angie was probably at the 6th Street Co-op. How the hell was he gonna tell her?

"Do you need a ride, Hun?"

Oh, Karen. The expression on her face brought it all home for him. She looked sympathetic, the way someone who heard such news should look. Maybe he should sit beside her and cry for a while, get it over with. But cry for Horst? Could he really ever picture himself doing that? He wanted to smoke a bowl and figure it out but he had to face Angie. She was the boss of the unit that was them, the monster's head, not him. Still, he knew that in a situation like this he would have to be there for whatever storm such news would bring up for her. All Angie's shit bubbled close to the surface. Sometimes he felt that he was the kind of person who had to be instructed what to feel, the way Karen's look was instructing him now. He fought it.

"No. I'm okay," he lied.

Karen reached out and ran her bar chapped fingers over his cheek the way she probably did with her son. He thought of his own mother.

"I'm sorry."

"It's just—weird."

"I'll get dressed. Give me two minutes?"

Zach noticed a faint ringing in his ears after she left the room. Something was happening to time, it seemed to both slow down and speed up concurrently. He found himself strangely aware of every minute as it passed. Maybe this is what grief felt like, he thought. He dressed quickly and ran a comb through his hair, catching his face in the mirror. All of his Horst-like features seemed to band together and push their way to the forefront. He never noticed them in so much stark detail before. Horst can't be dead, Zach thought, he's looking at me right now. He closed his eyes and shook off the feeling. It must have been the weed. When he opened his eyes again it was his own familiar image he saw, but something about it made him stop and wonder. If this was grief, why did he look so relieved?

When Zach got the call informing him of their father's death, Angie was lying jaybird naked on a painter's tarp in the middle of the 6th Street Co-op's chilly gallery floor, covered in a mixture of blue tempera paint and dish soap. The only part of her lithe, petite body that didn't belong in an amateur production of *Blue Man Group* was her face; her mouth was open, screaming with laughter, and she reeked of tequila.

The girl three feet to her right, another intern called Nikki, was in a similar, albeit more yellow predicament. To her left, Alex, a sculptress, was a horror show dripping in red. Sprawled on the ground, they resembled a trio of forest nymphs accidentally taken out during a renegade game of paintball. Above them, perched on a ladder was the photo artiste, El Oro, gazing lens down on his latest installation, working title: Color Wheel.

Spotted around the candlelit room in various stages of intoxication, consciousness, and undress, sat a sprinkling of turtle-necked spectators, hippie artists, and Westchester fashionistas, sipping wine and speaking in the hushed, reverent tones of the politely pretentious. The flash bulb from the ladder created a strobe light effect, giving the room a Lynchian aura that didn't go unnoticed.

Angie had been interning at the Co-op since September and was getting more then her fair share of education in the artist's life—that is to say, the artist's life as nocturnal, drunk and decadent. It suited her just fine.

"Reach out to her, Nikki. Caress her arm," the bearded artist instructed.

Angie looked drunkenly over at her new friend whose yellow hands on her blue arm managed to achieve an impressive, if not somewhat muddy, shade of green. There was a sprinkling of applause from the crowd.

"Now Angie, with your left hand," the photographer instructed with a pedophile's purr, "you caress Alex, no?"

Angie hesitated, weighing the artistic merits of the exercise. Blue mixed with red would make purple. She thrust a dripping arm in the direction of the red lady, severing her in two with a splash of color that bled a royal purple down her neck and breasts, the color of grapes. The audience gasped and Angie squealed. It was turning out to be quite a night.

The Co-op's monthly show and guest lectures were always followed by a cocktail hour that began innocently enough, but had an uncanny way of stretching all the way till dawn. It was the one night of the month that everyone looked forward to, especially the interns. They would spend all day setting up the show, buying the booze, making the hors d'oeuvres, and setting the stage for whatever artist du jour the board was able to coax to 6th Street. Being a Co-op, everyone got to show something, but they liked to place a jewel in the center of the crown, somebody who would play to the serious collectors and make the Co-op more than a fifty-dollar commission. That night it was Mexican photographer, El Oro, known for his photos of painted nudes.

By one in the morning the cocktail hour had morphed into a dance party, and El Oro offered to entertain the revelers with a floorshow installation. He chose Angie to model.

What was supposed to be a modest demonstration

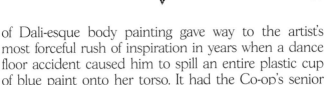

of Dali-esque body painting gave way to the artist's most forceful rush of inspiration in years when a dance floor accident caused him to spill an entire plastic cup of blue paint onto her torso. It had the Co-op's senior members scavenging the supply closets for materials to help him achieve his vision. It was all horribly exciting until, midway through the exercise, Angie realized that El Oro was excited in more ways than one.

She leaned over towards the red lady.

"Is it just me, or is that asshole pitching a tent?"

The girl turned away. It was impossible to tell whether or not she was blushing. Angie tried her jaundiced friend.

"Seriously, am I the only one who can see his—?"

"Angelina, get closer to Nikki, rub your thighs together," the artist drooled.

"Yeah, I bet you'd like that wouldn't you, Chubby Checker?"

Angie sprung to her feet and smashed back down an instant later. She made a mental note not to try and storm off a slippery plastic tarp while covered in paint and dish soap. Only slightly humiliated, she slid away on her bottom leaving a blue, slug-like trail that made the artist curse her in Spanish. Angie hoisted herself to her feet and stormed off leaving little, angry blue footprints all the way to the ladies room.

"Somebody bring me a fucking towel."

Freezing, annoyed, and still more than a bit drunk, Angie wiped away as much of the paint as possible while cursing loudly.

She thought mixing dish soap into the paint was supposed to make removing it easier. Still, one needs a shower to get rid of the stuff completely, she thought ruefully. When the towel had it, she slipped into a smock somebody left hanging on a nail behind the door and

✠

emerged looking like a refugee from the set of *Star Wars*.

She grabbed a bottle of tequila from behind the makeshift bar and found a seat in the back of the gallery under a wall of antique hand mirrors that she had helped hang that very morning. Each mirror was secured with a piece of chewing gum and illuminated with a tea light balancing on a matchbook underneath. Only about ten of the seventy tea lights still flickered. Angie lit her cigarette on one of them and watched as the flame sputtered away.

"Bang. You're dead," she whispered.

From her sulking point she could see her contribution to the art show cowering in the corner. Categorized as a sculpture, it was a steamer trunk wallpapered in wine labels. It had belonged to her mother and traveled with her parents to every major growing region on the planet. Some of the labels were from wine bottles more priceless then all the contents of all the galleries in the 6th Street Co-Op, not that anyone there would notice. People hardly knew it was a piece at all. Someone had even left a beer bottle on it.

Angie crawled over to the trunk, removed the offending longneck, and ran her fingers over the flaking labels. 1952 Chateau Larrivet Bordeaux, 1955 Barolo Giorgio Barbero, and the 1937 Chateau Mouton Rothschild. It was laughable to think what their worth would be today. She could only imagine what channels Horst had gone through to get them for her mother. Who he bribed, the lies he must have told, the criminals he undoubtedly paid off. They were unparalleled, even back in those days—and back in those days her father was not a rich man. Still, he would have done anything for Eve.

Suddenly the tequila didn't seem nearly as desirable. Angie put the bottle down, and as she did, felt a flutter in her stomach. Zach. She got up and went to the backdoor of the Co-op. Without hesitating she unlocked and opened it, letting in a gust of chilly autumn air and her brother.

"Where are we going?" Angie asked immediately. She could read him better then she could read herself but only to a certain point. Beyond breezy, transparent *Zach Valley* was the dark, imposing *Wall of Zach* and scaling that shit was hopeless.

"Why are you blue?" Zach asked in return.

"Come here." She closed the door and dragged him by the wrist into the front room where the installation had progressed into a full-fledged, girl-on-girl paint porno. The colors had blended so thoroughly that only brown was left.

"Were you mud wrestling?" Zach asked.

"No. I'm blue, see? I got out early."

Angie turned away from Zach and waved at El Oro. "Hey asshole," she shouted, "This is my husband the bounty hunter. Wanna come down here and tell him about your little 'art' installation?"

El Oro turned so quickly that he lost his footing and fell off the ladder, dropping his camera onto the cement floor. There was an eruption of noise in the crowd, at which point Zach decided it would be best to get them the hell out of there. He grabbed Angie by the waist and hoisted her up kicking and screaming.

"Fuck that fucker! I need my clothes, Zach."

"You have clothes at home, come on."

"Mom's trunk!"

"What?"

"We have to get Mom's steamer trunk, I'm not leaving it here."

Zach sighed.

"Where is it?"

Angie directed him to the trunk in the corner.

"Grab a side," she ordered, bending to lift it and

exposing her posterior to the wall full of hand mirrors.

"Go start the car. I'll get it." Zach tossed her the keys and sighed.

She flitted out into the night on bare feet while Zach did his brotherly duty. How in the world Angie had come to possess their mother's trunk was beyond him, but something about the presence of it made him queasy. He still had to tell her about Horst and lifting that trunk was a reminder of his sister's unyielding sentimentality towards the people her parents once were. It was also stealing apparently, as the trunk was part of the Co-op's art show.

"What do you think you're doing?"

Shit, thought Zach. Turtlenecks.

"Put that down, or we're calling the cops," shouted a man with a lisp.

Without thinking Zach made for the door, thrusting the trunk and himself out into the night towards the oncoming getaway car.

Angie threw open the passenger side door.

"Your party mobile, sir."

Because it was easier, he plopped the trunk down on the front seat and got in the back.

"Drive," he ordered.

Once they were on the highway Zach had her pull over and he took the wheel.

"Bounty hunter?"

"You could be a bounty hunter. It would be a great job for you. Really. That or pirate," Angie burped.

"Great. Um, Angie?" He should just come out and say it.
"Zach!"

"What?"

"Can you pull over? I gotta hurl."

While Angie showered Zach made them both tea

and smoked a bowl as the sky started to get light. He checked his e-mail and, as promised, there was a message containing the itinerary for two first class tickets to Seattle. From there Gabriel had arranged a private jet to take them to Lapis—to take them home.

Zach must have gotten lost in thought—something about Horst and a dirty linen pant leg—because when he went into the bedroom he found Angie curled up on his bed, sound asleep, still wrapped in a wet bath towel. He tossed the towel aside and pulled the covers over her, undressed himself, and climbed in beside her—his ball and chain, his other half.

He stroked his sister's damp hair and spooned up against her fragile, familiar form as he had countless times before, but not nearly recently enough. It had been months. Holding her was like recharging some kind of mysterious twin battery that whole people didn't have, need, or understand.

He picked at the blue paint that had dried stuck to her blonde roots, examining one strand at a time, mindlessly, like a monkey. They were a couple of monkeys. Hadn't Horst called them that? Now they were orphaned monkeys. He pictured the endangered wildlife poster that would feature such an image. Their little, sad-eyed faces pressed together as they cowered together in a lonely cage.

"Monkey?" He whispered.

"Hmm…?"

She was out. He could tell by the weight of her head on his arm. There was no tension, only oblivion.

"We have to go home today. Horst and Tilda died in a plane crash. We have to go deal with that, okay?"

"Mmm-hmm…."

"I need you to stay cool. I need you to help us get through this, Angel."

But she was off to tequila induced dreamland, doing

the Mexican Hat Dance with a mescal worm. If she heard him at all, the information had only been set adrift on the sea of her subconscious. Whatever tempest of emotion was over that horizon would have to wait until morning to make landfall. Zach held his sister tightly, battened down his own hatches, and braced them both for the storm to come.

CHAPTER THREE

3

3 · PULVERIZE ·

Zach woke up from a dreamless coma with the sun in his eyes and an empty bed. In those precious few seconds before the hangover hit, before his brain organized itself back into its modus operandi, he felt warm and noticeably content. It was as if the bed had swallowed him whole and consumed him completely, taking with it all vestiges of the night before and filing them under the heading of *bad dream*. But as the day fought its way in with little sounds and smells, the puzzle of his life came back into cruel focus, assaulting him with images that he couldn't escape. Reluctantly, he opened his eyes.

The first thing he saw was the steamer trunk. Now he remembered. It was one of the fuzzier details of the previous evening—them dragging it in, and Angie insisting that they keep it in his room. She said something about the labels being worth more than anything his Cro-Magnon roommates owned, and how it wasn't safe in the living room; the usual Angie drivel. But looking as it did in the morning light, diffused through the hundred-year-old windows of his Victorian house, the thing did hold a strange sort of magic. Even through sleep crusted eyes he was able to make out the details that few others would notice. Though the labels themselves were valuable perhaps only to a specialty collector, he understood something more. He knew that the trunk was a physical representation of a love that once thought itself immune to death.

The trunk lid was open. He wanted to look inside, but he also wanted to reach for the glass of water on his nightstand and neither seemed to be happening. Before he mustered the strength to raise his head and do either, he heard the door open and was hit by a wave of coffee-scented air. Zach turned his head and saw his mother Eve standing in the doorway. The only practical problem was that she'd been dead for sixteen years.

"Uncanny isn't it?"

Angie leaned on one hip in the doorway, gripping two mugs of coffee and wearing a dress that hadn't seen daylight since the Seventies. She was a vision in the clingy brown and orange sweater dress, and she nearly frightened Zach out of his skin.

"Holy fuck, Ange!" He wondered how it was possible for one person to be so flawlessly infuriating. Was there anything else she could have done to make what he had to tell her harder? Anything she could have said?

"Horst has a suit in there. Wanna play dress up?"

He had to tell her. He had to tell her now before the hole got any deeper. Sure she might scream, and rage, and cry, and make his life a miserable living hell, but having to lie there and look at her in Eve's dress for one more second was more then he could bear.

She sat on the bed and handed him a mug of coffee.

"Angie," he began, "We have to talk—"

"Oh, Horst and The Baroness kicked it last night. You better get dressed. We're goin' to Prosser."

She got up and practically danced into the kitchen, leaving Zach to pick his jaw up off the floor.

"What?"

She knew. She knew and this was her reaction? No tantrum? No nothing? He counted on her to be the emotional one. She was supposed to be upset enough for both of them. He was supposed to comfort her, not the other way around. Her apathy was unacceptable. Even worse, it put the burden back on him. Someone had to feel something. Someone had to freak out. Right?

He followed her like a zombie into the kitchen where she was in the middle of preparing breakfast. Bacon, eggs, toast—the whole shebang.

"I know, right. I got an e-mail from Gabe. Their plane went down over some island somewhere. Sharks. No gruesome business of bodies. Blah, blah. It was only a matter of time if you ask me. What did you want to talk about?"

But something wasn't right. She was squeezing oranges. Zach had never seen her squeeze oranges in their whole life. Maybe this was her way of dealing with things. Maybe, he reasoned, this was Angie in shock, like back in junior high school when Ashton Warren broke up with her and she knitted socks for every member of Horst's staff. Is that what this was?

Zach's surly, bearded, roommate Bob was sitting at the kitchen table engrossed in a year-old issue of *High Times*.

"You want some coffee, Bob?" Angie sang, and poured him some without waiting for an answer.

"Thanks Ange. Oh, and tell your dipshit brother I know what he did to *The Big Lebowski*," Bob grumbled.

Angie turned to Zach spatula in hand.

"Zachary, Bob is very cross with you for what you did to his *Big Lebowski* poster."

"The Dude is not pleased."

"See? The Dude is not pleased. How do you want your eggs?" She tilted her head to the side and scrunched up her nose. "Scrambled?"

"Angie, can I speak to you for a moment?"

"Shoot, bro. I'm pullin' a Rachel Ray over here though so you better talk fast. Hey Bob, you got any E-V-O-O?"

"I'm serious, Angie...."

Bob got up and started going through the cupboards for olive oil.

"All we got is Mazola."

"It was a joke, Bob." Angie turned to her brother. "Look, Zach, I know news like this can be very upsetting...."

"What news?" Bob had relocated to the fridge, his nose violating the pour spout on a carton of orange juice.

"Our father died," she stage whispered.

"Woah."

"But, we have to look at the situation rationally. We have four, no, three and a half hours till we have to be on a plane, which means we have to focus. Bob has agreed to drive us to the airport...."

"I have?"

"And if we want to be there on time we need to eat something now, pack, and be on the road in forty-five minutes. I've timed it all out. I don't have time to go home and pack, but luckily, Eve's clothes fit me so I'm all fuckin' set."

"Angie."

Zach watched her plate the food with the practiced, choreographed moves of a professional chef. It was worse than he thought. At some point he had managed to lose control of the reins. Now she had them and she wasn't letting go.

"Eat." She slapped his plate down on the table and garnished the fruit salad she had made with a fresh daisy.

"Don't order me around." Zach's voice was level and low.

"Fine. Don't eat. Starve. Oh, I'm sorry, was that an order as well? Okay, why don't you do whatever you want?"

"I don't want to fight."

"Good. Then sit down and eat your breakfast." Angie took her own advice and sat at the table, unfolding a paper towel and placing it daintily across her lap.

"I'm not hungry. I just found out my father died," Zach

said. It was a cheap shot, but true nonetheless. At that moment he could hardly stomach the thought of food.

Angie closed her eyes and took a deep breath.

"Bob, would you like Zach's breakfast?"

Bob probably did want it, having been stoned all weekend, but knew better then to look a coiled cobra in the eye.

"I'm gonna go in here," Bob said, pointing to the laundry room, and slinked away.

"Okay. You don't want it, he doesn't want it, I'll throw it out."

Angie took the rim of the plate tightly between her thumb and forefinger and thrust it across the room in the direction of the garbage can. It shattered on contact with the floor, the little daisy landing face down on a roach trap.

Zach turned and left the kitchen but Angie was right on his heels.

"That's it? Chilly silence? Or maybe you're grieving?" She pushed him hard, turning him around to face her. "You knew about this, Zachary. You knew last night and you didn't tell me. What the fuck is that about?"

"You were shit-faced, Angie."

"And you were getting your dick sucked by some geriatric road whore, so I'd hold off on the judgment if I were you."

Zach was dumbfounded. How could she possibly know about that? Were her twin powers getting stronger?

Angie went to the dining room table and picked up a bunch of convenience store daisies, handling them the way a Hazmat worker would handle a severed arm, with a mixture of pity and disgust. She glanced at the card.

"*Karen* sends her condolences." She threw the bouquet at him with all her might, and slowly, brick by brick, the dam began to come apart. "She came by early this morning to give you those. I thought it was a joke.

'Tell him I'm really sorry about his father,' she said."

"Oh, Ange…."

'I found out that Horst is dead from a total fucking stranger." She melted into the floor. "Do you have any idea…?"

She lost her words after this and the sobs came in heart-wrenching chokes. Zach knelt beside her. He buried his face into the back of her neck. Her skin was hot and smelled like mold from the dress. I'm sorry, was all he could say, over and over again, between each of her cries until the two of them fell into a kind of rhythm, his apologies rising and falling to match the intensity of her sobs.

On the living room floor they melded into each other, officially becoming one being, one sobbing apologizing mass, and when Angie guided Zach's hand to the cool of her thigh with the slightest touch, it was as if she were moving her own. The hand knew what to do. It pulled back the itchy fabric of the thirty-year-old dress and dug its nails into the soft, cool flesh just below the place where her hip met her thigh. In long steady strokes it rubbed slowly down to her knee with just enough force to leave welts in her skin, breaking the capillaries into tiny blood-filled bubbles that rose to the surface without breaking through. And again. And again. Ten, fifteen times, before Angie's breathing slowly returned to normal.

She took his head between her hands and silently kissed away his tears. They would be okay now.

"We should probably make a stop at my place, I need to pack." She got up without another word and drifted silently into his bedroom, closing the door behind her. It wasn't unusual for her to withdraw after episodes like that; it had been her way since childhood.

Zach noticed Bob liberating himself from the laundry room in a cloud of reefer smoke. Zach wondered how much he had seen.

✦

"How you doin' man? You want some of this?" Bob asked, offering a spliff.

Zach took a hit and clapped Bob on the back.

"I guess I better take care of that mess in the kitchen."

Like a good friend, Bob assisted him, munching on Angie's leftovers, and by eleven that morning they were on their way to Albany to catch their flight.

From car, to airport, to airplane, Angie seemed to glide, gazing out of windows, lost in thought. She hardly spoke, and when she did it was to inform Zach of tertiary information—like when she had to use the bathroom, or to remind him not to forget their passports. Once the plane took off she was asleep with her head propped uncomfortably against the cabin wall. Zach had ordered them each a Bloody Mary, drank both, and relocated her head to his shoulder. A flight attendant passed by.

"Does your wife need a blanket?" she whispered.

"Actually she's…." Zach glanced over at Angie. Her hands were in her lap, palms up as though she were cradling empty space. Her little finger twitched. She had a hole in her tights. His love for her was total. It spanned the gamut from indifference to obsession. If he ever did marry, it would probably kill her. The flight attendant was hot, if he told her the truth he could flirt without looking like a scumbag. She's not my wife she's my sister. Go on. Say it.

"Yes. A blanket would be great."

He watched a movie, he watched the news, he watched Angie, and sat through the minutes as they passed, feeling each one like marbles lodged in an hourglass. Five hours later they touched down in Seattle, by nightfall they would be home.

4 · SUBLIME ·

The private jet touched down on a small airstrip just outside Prosser at about six-thirty in the evening. The sky was sporting every imaginable color in a display that showcased nature at her most whorish: blues and pinks, oranges and purples. The only color not present was green, a faux pas that the surrounding fields more than compensated for. Zach took in a lungful of crisp, clean air. There was nothing subtle about it; he was home.

A town car waited for them on the tarmac, luggage was shuffled, people were tipped, and within a frenzied few minutes Zach and Angie found themselves in the back seat barreling towards Lapis Vintners.

Angie was in better spirits after her five-hour nap, and she had slipped into a mood Zach characterized as softly melancholy. She was being sweet to him, which was a relief. If only he didn't know her so well. If he wasn't aware that these moods were as fragile as flash paper, maybe then he would be able to relax.

"I'm famished," she said, letting her head roll to the side. Her hair without any product in it looked like a horse's mane, it fell in soft black and blonde curls over her hazel eyes. "Maybe we should stop and pick up some groceries in case Gabriel forgot."

"Ange, it's Lapis. There's enough food up there to feed a small army."

"I don't want migrant food. Come on, Zach, you know what I mean."

He did know. And she was right; there probably wouldn't be any food in the main house if Gabriel hadn't gone shopping. And why would he? He ate with the workers. And now that Horst and Tilda were no longer there….

"Driver, would you mind making a stop at Food Depot? It's on Market Street."

"Sorry, Mr. Bartlett. I have to get you both to Kestrel before seven."

"Kestrel?" Angie sat upright. "We're not going to Kestrel, we're going to Lapis."

Angie's fuse had been lit. Zach could sense her bristling as she turned to look at him with one eye raised, but he just shrugged in return. Kestrel, Lapis, they were just next door to each other anyway.

"My dispatcher was very specific. Kestrel by seven sharp."

"Who called it in?" Zach leaned forward with both hands on the driver's seat.

"The name on my sheet is Gabriel Gurerro. Have a look." The driver handed Angie the clipboard with the pick-up time and drop-off location.

"See?" said Zach. "If it was Gabriel, I'm sure he had a reason."

"I can call base if you want," the driver offered.

Angie handed him the clipboard back.

"No, it's okay," she said and turned toward Zach. "They'll probably have some decent food at Kestrel."

Angie slumped back into her seat and watched out the window as the sky over I-82 turned from magenta to lavender.

"Pretty isn't it? I wish I could paint. I'd paint the Prosser sky for everyone I know back east. They'd never believe it."

Soft Angie. He put his hand over hers but she pulled away in order to rub her thigh. He read volumes into this gesture and wished he didn't. He wished he didn't care so much, he wished he'd swallowed her in the womb that way he could carry her inside himself and protect her forever.

The town car pulled up in front of Kestrel Vintners a few minutes before seven o'clock. The parking lot was full and the place was lit up like Qwest Field. Prosser was in the middle of the fall crush and it looked like they had arrived on the night of Kestrel's harvest kickoff party.

Married couples swung their linked hands together. A group of girls featuring a veiled, bride-to-be bounced happily towards impending oblivion. And the Seattle intellectuals in their corduroy jackets and Norma Kamali dresses hung back discussing how cultural events like this one had been ruined by any number of things, all stemming from the national media.

The twins emerged from the car looking like a couple of chewed up vampires that had been spat out onto the pavement. They were dressed head to toe in black, pasty pale with bloodshot eyes. A girl in a gingham dress skipped by holding a basket filled with fine cheeses.

"What the fuck are we doing here?" Angie asked.

For once Zach shared her sentiment to a tee. He turned to the driver who was dutifully unpacking their things from the trunk.

"Listen man, I'm gonna need you to take us to Lapis after all. It's just up the road…." Zach pulled out his wallet with plans to exorbitantly tip the guy when he heard a familiar voice.

"Zach, Angie!"

Kat Slater? Kat, fucking, tight-abs Slater? He couldn't help but smile. His high school dream girl bounced towards them on five-hundred dollar heels, her pilates body practically poured into a designer suit. She had the same golden skin and shining hair. Macedonian vanilla, a thin musky layer—not too much, not too little—surrounded her like an aura. Zach handed the driver a fifty. The guy thanked him and started putting their bags back in the car.

"Where do you think you're going?" Kat smiled.

"Kat? Oh my God." As they hugged, Zach was able to catch a glance of Angie, not that he couldn't already feel her energy sucking at him like a black hole. She was stone faced.

"Hi Angie." Kat went in for a hug but got little in return. "I'm so sorry you guys."

"What are you doing here, Kat?" Angie asked, her words void of emotion.

"Angie, come on." Zach was reading too much into her words and knew it as soon as the correction left his lips. She shot him an icy look.

"No, it's okay, Zach. It's a valid question." Kat tossed her hair, drowning him in a wave of her scent. "I'm working. You know—if you can call drinking wine and mingling *work.*"

"You work for Kestrel now?" Zach tried to act as though he wasn't caught in her tractor beam but he wasn't fooling anybody.

"Oh God, no. I only mean that they're a client. I represent most of the local vintners now."

"Are you a lawyer?"

"Yeah, Zach. She graduated high school five-and-a-half years ago and she's a lawyer," Angie quipped.

Zach tried to play it off. "It must be the jet lag," he said, blushing slightly.

"I'm a realtor actually. And vice chair of the Prosser Development Fund. Just a little committee to raise the region's profile on a national level, bring in some outside investors, that type of thing. We're working on a project that requires a certain amount of market research… but, it's boring, I can tell you more about it later."

"Yeah. Can't wait. We gotta go." Angie gave a half-assed grin and got back in the car.

"Go? What do you mean go? You just got here."

"Zach?" Angie scratched at the hole in her tights, impatient.

"Look, guys, I know how hard this must be for you, but through that door is a whole room full of people who loved your father very much and they really want to see you."

"Is Gabriel here?" Zach asked.

"Yeah."

"And Flint?" Angie watched Zach bristle. She wasn't the only one who got jealous.

"Of course. It's his event."

"Fine." Angie got out of the car and closed the door behind her. "Ten minutes. Zach, tell the driver to wait." She stormed off towards the winery, leaving Kat and Zach behind.

"You have to forgive her, she's upset. It's been a pretty messed up twenty-four hours."

Kat smiled a honeyed smile and gave her eyelashes a bat. Her expression was oozing with sympathy.

"Some things never change. I don't think that sister of yours ever liked me. But you did, right Zach?"

"That's a silly question."

"I'm glad you feel that way. I always liked you too. God…," Kat paused, raising her hands to frame Zach's face the way a movie director might. "You look so much like your father. He was a client of mine too."

"Really?"

"Oh yes. He was such a nice man. I'll come by Lapis soon and walk you through some of the plans he had for the place."

"Plans? He wasn't thinking of selling was he?"

"Let's talk about it in a few days."

"He would never sell Lapis, Kat. Not in a million years."

Zach peeled off another fifty for the driver and followed Kat inside. There were a few people congregating in the shop but most had gone down the hall to the tasting room to listen to Flint speak. When Zach and Kat walked in everyone seemed frozen, glasses in the air, examining the color of small lot, wild yeast Chardonnay.

Master winemaker, Flint Nelson led the tasting.

Flint. He had come to Prosser the year before the twins left for college to take over the reins at Kestrel. Flint was an artisan winemaker with loads of talent, a good reputation, and a brilliant gift for Yakima Valley fruit. He was also handsome to a fault, kind to children, a lover of animals, and he recycled. There was little not to like about the guy, and Zach couldn't help but hate him.

Flint was well-known in Prosser. During his last year at Washington State Flint had apprenticed under Horst for a season. Zach was a regular sixteen-year-old boy at the time and Angie was *Lolita*. Flint was her first crush and she followed him around like a drooling puppy that whole summer. Some nights she would fall asleep outside the door to his shack and have to be carried home in the morning covered in dust and fire ants. Flint would call her kiddo when he wasn't trying to avoid her, which was most of the time.

After he found her naked in his bed on more than one occasion, Flint decided to speak to Horst about the problem. They did the sensible thing, and Flint went back to the university two weeks early. Angie wept until Christmas.

For her, Flint was like a cancer—he had his remissions but never really went away. So when he returned to Prosser ten years later, married to a lovely lady winemaker, Angie had a relapse that ended with a razorblade, a bathtub, and a 911 call placed by the twin brother who found her. It was the final incident that tipped Horst in favor of letting the twins go to Bard—out of sight out of mind, he figured. No one was told, and life went on.

Angie hadn't seen Flint in five-and-a-half years and now she was sitting beside him while he spoke. Her wine sat forgotten on the table while she gazed up at him. Zach had to get her out of there.

"Zach, what's wrong?"

"I have to take Angie home. Where's Gabriel?"

Kat looked over and saw what Zach was referring to.

"Oh that? I wouldn't worry about that."

"You don't understand."

"Actually, I do. Your father told me what happened."

"He did? And you don't see the problem?"

"Once the two of you get back to Lapis, you're going to be too busy for such childish distractions. But then again, maybe you do have a point. Some crushes die hard."

Zach felt her hand on the small of his back. He pulled away.

"Excuse me."

Zach made his way through the tables to where Angie was sitting.

"Come on, Ange. Let's go."

But it was too late; Flint had seen him and stopped his oratory.

"Zachary, I'm so sorry to hear about your father. Horst taught me everything I know about the Yakima Valley. He will be sorely missed."

"Thanks Flint. We um, we were looking for Gabriel. Have you seen him?"

Flint poured a taste of Chardonnay for Zach as part of some polite, robotic, second nature.

"Not tonight. I doubt he's here after everything that's

happened. I hear there's quite a bit to be done, signatures and such that frankly… well, wouldn't that kind of thing need your attention?"

"Yeah. We have a car waiting outside. Come on, Ange."

"We should toast him first," Flint said.

"Yes, a toast," Angie sighed.

Was that an English accent Zach heard?

Something weird happened to Angie in the presence of Flint. It was as if all the air went out of her and her bones turned to slush. Just days before she cut her wrists she told Zach that she would gladly trade her life for the life of Flint's dog. She said she could picture no greater happiness in the world then sitting at Flint's feet, following him around all day, and eating his table scraps. It was a scenario that made Zach want to vomit then strangle her.

"All right," Zach agreed.

Flint tapped the handle of his bread knife against the side of his glass. "Everyone, we have a pair of guests tonight, Angelina and Zachary Bartlett. Their father, Horst Bartlett, and his wife, Tilda, were tragically killed in a plane crash just the other evening. Angelina would like to make a toast."

Angie sprung up and whispered something in Flint's ear in a lightning fast move that put both Zach, and Flint's wife Emma, on a quick offensive. But Angie sat down before anyone could move. No harm, no foul.

"On second thought, Angelina would like me to make the toast. So I say, to Horst Bartlett. A good man and a genius winemaker. I apprenticed under him many, many, moons ago and he taught me many things, but if I had to pick one—one little lesson that lives with me to this very day…well, it's not little. It's a philosophy that I strive towards in everything I do here at Kestrel. Horst had his secrets, his tricks of the trade, as we all do, but for him, at its core, winemaking was about consistency.

And consistency means doing what works over and over again. It means paying attention throughout the entire process: growing, harvesting, picking, fermentation, aging, blending, filtrations and bottling. Each step is wrought with potential pit-falls. If you're not paying attention things can go terribly astray. Horst knew this and he dedicated his life to the perfection of this process. Winemaking was more than a job to him, it was an art. This region and the industry as a whole will suffer for the loss. Let's all raise our glasses—to Horst."

"To Horst."

Now they were stuck. After the toast, people lined up to pay their respects. They were local growers and business associates who had known Horst and Tilda, many were finding out the bad news for the first time. Zach and Angie handled the receiving line with dignity and grace. By the end they had a stack of business cards, in case they needed anything at all, and for when they arranged the official memorial service, just call, please call.

Flint saw them to the car personally.

"Hang in there guys."

What a dick, Zach thought.

Angie sighed as Flint walked away. Then she took in a deep breath and her bones became solid again.

"What happened to Malibu Barbie?"

"Kat? I don't know."

"She's playing some kind of fucking game, Zach. Gabe had fuck-all to do with us going to Kestrel. He wasn't even there. I'll bet you cold hard cash that Kat ordered this car in his name. And I bet she did it just so she could see you."

A minute or two later Angie would get the bright idea of having the driver radio his dispatcher to find out whether the person who called in the order for the car was male or female. Two or three minutes after that, the dispatcher radioed back to say that the caller was indeed female but left the name Gabriel Gurerro.

Still, all of this was mere confirmation of what Zachary knew all along. Angie was right; Kat ordered the car, but not only as an excuse to see him. Something in his gut was telling him that she did it for another reason. That she might have done it so Angie would see Flint.

5·RECEIVER·

The town of Prosser, Washington is nestled in a parabola formed by the Yakima River. An enabler of the grand Columbia, its waters trickle down from the western mountains and weave a path through the rocky valley. This is not the Washington of the coast. Those expecting the soaked green, sponge-like atmosphere usually associated with the Pacific Northwest will find they have been misled by assumption.

Prosser is rattlesnake country. It owes its very existence to the river, and its agricultural success to the modern marvels of irrigation. It is a barren valley turned by man into nature's work camp. Pear trees stand in line with apple trees, corn stalks line up ear-to-ear, and grape vines, in perhaps the cruelest bondage of all, hang pruned and exposed in the glaring sun off miles of rigid trellis wires.

Horst Thannhauser and his young wife Eve Bartlett arrived in Prosser in 1982 with her last name on their marriage license, a decision made as a romantic ode to its etymology, St. Bartholomew, the patron saint of vintners. They made their way up to Washington from San Francisco where they had met a few years earlier. It was a different life for both of them then, when he was a European backpacker living out his fantasies of America, and she was a former teenage runaway who dreamt of a quiet place to call home.

According to legend, Horst arrived in San Francisco in the summer of '78 without a pot to piss in, but only because he had purposely left said pot back in Germany with the tyrannical father he was trying to escape. While begging for change on Haight Street like a common panhandler—a concept he secretly adored—he met an angel. She was a young straw-haired flower child by the name of Eve. Within days he was on his knees begging to be her Adam. Within weeks they were married.

After the wedding they banded together with five other lost flower children and traveled north, picking up migrant work as they went. In Sonoma, Napa, Lodi, and Mendocino, Horst and Eve found solace among the grape vines they tended, often losing themselves for days at a time in the rows of nurtured vines. Eve loved their order, their reliability, the simplicity of their existence, and above all, their reliance on her. The vines she tended became her children and with Horst at her side she absorbed every fact she could that would help her care for them best. She was a strange kind of prodigy, and her skill didn't go unnoticed by her employers. Every season they welcomed the arrival of the pretty blonde and the hulking German who seemed to have a way with the grapes.

After four seasons in California, they bid farewell to their original group and let their curiosity take them north to wind up in Columbia, Washington. Work was scarce and they were unknown, so they followed a tip which landed them in Prosser. After a week of bad luck they were about to cash in the remainder of their dwindling chips and head back south, but in a stroke of luck, the hitchhiking couple happened upon an untended field and sought out the owner to offer their assistance.

The old man who owned the place, Gregory Phibes, had been harvesting and selling whatever wild grapes he could pull out of his fields for years. Horst and Eve, seeing the opportunity in this, offered their services for a nominal fee and within three years had tamed Phibes Winery from a wilderness into a thriving business. When the old man died he left the place to the couple, dubbing them the children he never had.

On the night they took ownership, they made love in the field. Horst renamed the winery Lapis after the ancient philosopher's stone, the holy grail of the alchemist. It was their child now, said Eve, a new birth. Horst ran his hand over the soft skin of her stomach and agreed. For what was winemaking without the powers of transmutation?

If one were to visit Lapis today it would mean crossing the Yakima via the Grant Avenue Bridge and continuing northward on Old Inland Empire Highway until it turns into Hinzerling Road. Lapis Drive snakes its way west through tailored rows of grape vines and ends at a giant, Gothic, wrought iron gate with a scripted *L* welded into it like a cattle brand.

The main house sits imposingly at the end of a long straight drive. Built to resemble a southern plantation, it appears stark and white without any of the edge-softening foliage usually accompanying such architecture. Its weathered columns stretch from patio to roof and wrap around the house completely, allowing each balcony a view of the vineyard.

The architect, as far as anyone could gather, was a wealthy descendent of Smith Barnum. Before the land was irrigated for farming, it was home to herds of cattle. The rancher who owned the land, a transplant from the southeast by the name of Royer, hired a young Barnum to build him a house with a wrap around patio and a widow's walk so he could keep a constant eye out for poachers. The design had worked well for his father in Raleigh, Royer explained. From that height he never lost one slave.

The result of Royer's inherited paranoia was the massive, structural anomaly that Horst etched, printed, and slapped on every bottle of Lapis wine. A ghostly structure rising from the dusty valley, book-ended on either side by fantastically tailored rows of twisted vine.

Outside of the picturesque frame of the main house sat the barn, a rust-colored, cedar-lined behemoth, converted into a modern tasting room in front, and an attractively vast, barrel storage space in the back. Most of the local vintners had their tasting rooms closer to town, but as Horst liked to boast, Lapis remained one of the few onsite operations.

Past the barn was another dirt road that led to the migrant shacks. Like the barn and the house, they came with the land, but were so dilapidated that Horst had them fully renovated in the early 90's. The two facing rows of nondescript shacks became a lively village under Horst's care. Horst was known for his generosity to his employees, and for his lack of restrictions when it came to his little "pueblo."

Horst hired whole families, the men to work the fields, the women to cook and run the village—he even hired a teacher for the children, his own included, and encouraged music whenever possible. The twins spoke fluent Spanish as children, and for a time, with more skill than their English.

For Eve and Horst, the pueblo was the sweetest part of their operation. Although the concept was never addressed directly, there was a certain light in Eve's eyes when Horst found her conversing with the women, mindlessly folding cornhusks into tamales, or hanging laundry to dry in the midday sun, her hair falling across her smile. Lapis had fulfilled her dreams of utopia.

But time changes everything, and when Eve died, the pueblo died with her. The migrants were all men now, men whom Gabriel was constantly having to police for vice. He was doing just that when the twins arrived home. One of the workers had brought a woman back to his shack and some of the others were complaining about the noise. Gabriel had dealt with it the way he dealt with everything: with careful consideration of what Horst would do.

Gabriel let himself quietly into the house. There was a change of energy when the twins came home. It reminded him of simpler times, when the family was young, when there was a center to things that could be easily pinpointed. He glided softly down the hall, avoiding by nature the noisy floorboards that had driven Tilda into fits of nerves. He could hear the twins in the study. He tapped lightly on the door.

Angie knew that knock. She also knew Gabriel wouldn't come in unless he was invited. "Come in," she said.

The door swung open revealing the Salvadorian beanpole that was Gabriel Gurerro. She had asked him once—she must have been about seven—if he was her father's slave. The question prompted a pinch on the ear and a lecture about the Civil War from Horst, but she never forgot the look on Gabriel's face. She had her answer. They all worshiped *Father Bartlett* back then. Well, most of them anyway.

Gabriel and Zach shook hands the way they always did, with a clap on the back that was almost a hug but wasn't. Angie greeted him in her usual fashion as well, wrapping her arms around his neck and planting two inappropriately long kisses on both cheeks. Ever the stoic, Gabriel stared unblinking at the wall across the room, only relaxing slightly when she released him.

"Welcome home," Gabriel began. His soft South American purr was unusually strained. He looked like he'd been up all night. "I'll make this easy. There's business, papers that need to be signed, a couple of creative decisions that were never made concerning the new Merlot labels. I can take care of this if you like. The little things will take two, three days, at most. Due to the nature of the accident there are no remains, so no burial is necessary. A memorial can be arranged for now, after the crush, never—it's your decision." Gabriel sat and rubbed at his temples. "The bigger questions, you have time. Either you sell or you don't sell. If you don't sell, we can run it without you. If you want to run it, come home. Again—your decision."

There was a mournful silence while they processed his words before Angie decided to lasso the white elephant standing in the corner of the room with her usual tact.

"He didn't leave you anything, did he?"

Gabriel grinned a tired grin.

"He gave me the last thirty years of my life. He owes me nothing."

Angie thought for a second.

"Yeah, sorry Gabe, but that's *bullshit*."

"Angie, settle down," Zach pleaded.

"Oh, come on, Zachary. That was a dick move. He didn't leave Gabriel anything? Not even like a percentage of something, or *something*?" She got up and began pacing the floor under a giant portrait of Tilda with a death grip around a Pomeranian. "See? This is what I mean. He was a fucking cheap bastard, emotionally, monetarily, with people, and that's exactly why everybody thinks he's so great—that's how he gets you. That's his game. He's like a drug dealer; you get just enough Horst to keep you coming back for more. But ask for more, and you get shit on. Gabe, you're the one who gave. You gave your life to him, he took it, and he has you thanking him? He's a succubus. And she," Angie thrust a finger in the direction of Tilda's portrait, "she was a fucking vampire. They were perfect for each other and frankly, I'm glad they're dead. You can have this place, Gabe. Even better, lets burn it all down and split the insurance money. I'm going to bed."

She stormed out. Zach and Gabriel followed the sound of her footsteps on the stairs, down the hall, and finally to the bedroom, her words punctuated by the anticipated slam of her door. Zach and Gabriel exchanged a look; they were in this together now.

"Come with me," Gabriel said.

Zach grabbed his coat and followed Gabriel through the kitchen and out the back door. They boarded a golf cart, an eight-seater with the Lapis logo printed on the side. Tilda had gotten it for Horst as a Christmas present the previous year so they could give tours of the vineyards. She called it his *surrey with the fringe on top,* which unilaterally annoyed everybody. Was she as bad as Angie said, or just different, maybe? Zach didn't know. He didn't know anything. He was a man of no opinion, a walking gray area, an elephant in a world of zebras.

A chilly few minutes later they passed the barn and turned down a dusty stretch of road that led to the Lab, a stainless steel structure built by Horst to house the fermentation vats. Gabriel hopped out and unlocked the industrial strength padlock that secured the sliding steel doors. Metal scraped against metal with a sound that echoed over the fields. Gabriel disappeared into the dark, and a moment later the overhead lights flickered on in rows with an electrical hum, revealing what had always made Zach think of a cryogenics facility for giants.

The huge stainless steel fermentation vats simmered away, yeast busy eating sugar and secreting alcohol at its own steady pace.

"Where are they at?" Zach asked.

"Most of them just went in, three, four days. This one just yesterday. But here, have a look at this."

Gabriel led Zach to the vat at the end of the row. He placed a glass under the sample valve capturing a precise amount of virgin wine. After swirling it and examining the color closely, he handed it to Zach.

"We're racking this one off first thing in the morning. A Chardonnay. It has amazing potential. It was one of your father's last efforts."

"One of?" Zach asked, bringing his nose to the wine.

"Well yes, it's the Merlot that will be the jewel of the season. It's only been in the vat four days though."

"Gabriel, you're holding out on me. You think you're the only one with the gift of foresight?" Zach smiled and handed the glass back to Gabriel without tasting it. "I'd get this out tonight if I were you. Wait till morning and you're gonna be sorry."

Gabriel sipped from the glass and nodded. Zach was right.

"Over here. Your father's final Merlot."

He performed the same ritual and handed Zach a glass of unfermented wine.

The wine hit his lips and Zach's knees buckled. It tasted like, well, grape juice. But somewhere beyond that, below that, and above it too—young love, a first kiss, a broken heart….

"Gabriel, I can't do this. I'm not capable of…."

"You're his son."

Zach was overwhelmed with doubt and exhaustion. Nothing in his life made sense in that moment, but when it came to the wine swirling in his glass, he was sure of its perfection beyond a shadow of a doubt. When it came to wine, Zach knew right where he belonged.

CHAPTER 6

SIX

6 · FUMES ·

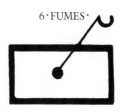

Angie opened her jet-lagged eyes at twenty-past-eleven and was greeted by an irritating concept unfolding around her. Daylight filled her childhood bedroom with shafts of golden sun, and as her lazy eyes traced the room's perimeter she couldn't help but notice that it was exactly as she had left it the previous Christmas. Exactly. The winter coat left on the back of her desk chair in favor of the new one she got from The Baroness still hung carelessly there. An abandoned coffee mug sat on her nightstand lined with brown goo and her balled up Santa socks, a joke gift from Zach, still lurked at the foot of the bed, twisted beyond all recognition. Not a soul had so much as stepped foot in her room in just under a year, not even for the coffee mug, which she knew full well was part of a set. Out of sight, out of mind, she figured. They probably closed the door on the day she went back to school, lit some sage to clear the air of her, and celebrated. But, fuck 'em, Angie thought, no use wasting energy on the dead.

She propped up her pillows and had a good long stare out the French doors onto the vineyard. Her room was on the east side of the house, which in her opinion provided the loveliest view. The gentle south-facing slope of the field coming off the mountains was interrupted only by the barn before continuing gracefully out to Hinzerling Road. When she stood up she could also see the Lab, which was an eyesore, but from the bed the view was picture perfect. Angie lay where she was and watched little clouds cast their shadows over portions of the field, making it resemble the spotted back of a cow. Beauty was Prosser's grip. Jesus Christ, she had to get out of there.

Angie showered, dressed, and made her way down to the huge, sun-soaked kitchen only to find the room and the coffee maker empty. She made a new pot and did a quick shouting sweep of the house for Zach. No luck. It wasn't hard to lose someone at Lapis. Cell phone reception was rare at best and Horst's walkie-talkie system never really caught on. Zach was probably in the barn, Angie thought. If not, the Lab was the next place to check. If he wasn't there, he might have gone into town with Gabe, and then again they might always be in the field, and good fucking luck finding them if that was the case.

Angie poured herself a cup of sugary coffee and wrapped a ruby-red pashmina that could only have been Tilda's, around her shoulders. As an added bonus she noticed a Louis Vuitton sunglass case lying on the kitchen counter and helped herself to its expensive, French contents. What? It was sunny. She would try the barn. If Zach wasn't there she was going back to bed.

It was a beautiful fall day, warm in the sun with only the slightest hint of a chill if you found yourself standing in a shadow. Somewhere in the valley someone was burning leaves, a smell Angie loved.

She could hear a steady banging coming from the barn and found Gabriel on a ladder hanging a banner from one of the rafters that read, *Got a Fall Crush?*

"Gabe?"

Gabriel stopped hammering and looked at her.

"Good morning, Angelina."

The banner floated to the ground like an angel wing. Gabriel climbed down to retrieve it.

"Sorry," she said, without moving a muscle to help him. "Have you seen, Zach?"

"He's in the Lab overseeing some bottling."

"Oh, is he now?"

"We have an event tonight."

"Oh, do we now? Even in light of recent—events?" She sauntered over to him and propped one arm on the ladder, blocking him from it.

"I suppose we could cancel but the advertisements have been up for weeks. It's an open tasting. No reservations, so I cannot call people to…."

"You could lock the gate. Turn that pretty banner of yours around and spray paint the words 'go away' on the back. That would do it," she sniped.

Gabriel removed his hat and scratched at the back of his head.

"You're right. Angelina, I'm sorry. It was insensitive of me to…."

Angie smiled and chucked him on the shoulder.

"Oh come on, Gabie. I'm just yanking your chain. Hang your faggoty banner. The show must go on right?" She smiled and spun on her heel, just missing his face with the whip of her borrowed pashmina. Without warning, Gabriel's hand caught her arm above the elbow in an iron grip.

"Hey," she said, trying to free herself.

"Where…," he began and stopped. Quickly he let go of her, glancing reflexively at the hammer still in his right grip. Angie saw his knuckles tense white against his skin before they relaxed.

"My apologies, Angelina," he said. "I am tired and there is much to do. You should go now and I will work."

He looked at the ground by his feet, and then at the ladder behind her. Anywhere but her face. Angie touched her arm where his hand had been and it was tender.

"Yeah, sure," she said.

As she left the barn, she turned once to look back at him, but he was hunched over the banner, nothing in his posture to suggest any concern about her presence. She shook her head. It was still early. Maybe she could still find Zach and convince him to split with her before they became as looney as everyone else in Prosser.

A few minutes later, she found Zach in the Lab where Gabriel said he would be, plying the family trade with shaking hands. He and a few others were in the process of stirring the wine, adding the sulfites and the fining agents, and finally filling the bottles to be corked. Zach oversaw the process in what Angie could only guess was a way of controlling his grief. Whether he could admit it to himself or not, Zach was grieving, of that she was sure. Horst had been an asshole to him over the years, but there was something about their relationship that she always secretly envied. Some lame father and son connection that she couldn't hope to understand. A spike of fear cut into her all of a sudden. If she wasn't careful she could lose Zach to it.

"What up, hermano?"

Zach turned quickly as if he had been caught with his hand in the cookie jar.

"Oh. Hey, Ange." He put down a bottle he was in the process of examining and backed away slightly. "Did you just get up?"

"Pretty much. What ya doin?" She picked up the bottle from where he left it and spun it in her hand.

"Chardonnay?"

"Yeah. Hey, which label do you like better?"

He offered her two sheets of paper each printed with a sample label. She put her hands up and backed away.

"Don't drag me into this, Zach."

"What do you mean? I just want your opinion. Come on, which one?"

She gave the artwork in Zach's hands a quick glance. They were two identical renderings of the plantation house with embossed text in slightly different layouts.

"That one. No, neither. I don't know…."

"What?"

"It's just—it's boring. It's the same stupid label they've been doing for years. Would it have killed Horst to punch it up a bit?"

Angie crossed her arms and waited for the reprimand, but Zach just nodded.

"You're right."

"Thank you."

"You should design one."

"Fuck that."

"No really, Ange. We have to be here for a couple of days. And we like, *own* this place now. We might as well act like it," Zach leaned closer and lowered his voice to a whisper, "for the sake of the staff."

"For the sake of the staff?" She said loudly with sarcasam.

Zach had a glimmer in his eye that Angie didn't like one bit. It was that Norman Rockwellian haze that always began to creep over people's faces after they fell under the spell of Prosser.

"All right, fine. I'll design a label if it makes you happy, but I get to do whatever I want, and you have to come to breakfast with me, in town, now."

Town, she thought, town would remind him firsthand what a shit-hole Prosser was. Maybe they could take a detour past the potato processing plant.

"I'll drive," she practically sang.

"But we still have all this bottling to—"

She shot him a look and he dutifully followed her out the door, well aware of the workers' mocking grins that trailed behind him.

Later that afternoon Zach went back to the Lab to work and Angie, who had already hit an almost critical boredom, decided to take advantage of the afternoon sun on her father's widow's walk. In order to get there she had to pass through his and Tilda's bedroom and take the ladder from Horst's private office. It was a journey she had not made in quite some time. She put on a bikini, grabbed a towel, her headset, and headed to their bedroom door.

It was ajar. Someone had drawn the curtains, sinking the bedroom into an eerie midday hibernation. Angie threw open the door and moved confidently across the rug as if it were no big deal, even taking a moment to look around to prove she could handle the weirdness. The four-poster bed was perfectly made and everything was put in its place. It felt like a hotel suite or a department store showroom, with none of the human touches that might rile the emotions of a grieving onlooker. It was almost as if no one had died at all, because no one could have possibly lived in this room, not really. Where was Horst's neglected coffee cup? Where were Tilda's rolled up Santa socks? No, they both went neatly and orderly to their watery graves just as cold and detached as they had been in life.

Beyond the antique chaise was the door to Horst's office. How it had terrified her as a child. Being inside Horst's office meant trouble, reprimands, and punishments. Only a handful of other occasions were remembered fondly. Those were the times that she and Zach cut through the office to stargazing or to observe the harvest from the widow's walk, their heads bent near each other, hands clasped tightly as though they were one unit.

Angie turned the knob, half hoping it would be locked, but it wasn't. She pushed open the door and flipped the light switch. Suddenly she felt eight-years-old again. It was exactly as she had remembered it. A windowless tomb lined with glass-incased bookshelves. In the center was his giant mahogany desk and worn leather chair. The fireplace on the wall immediately to her right was double-sided to serve both the office and the bedroom, providing a crafty child a full view of the beating her brother was receiving while she waited her turn, or vice versa. And, of course, there was the painting. *The Blood of Christ.*

It frightened her more then anything else. She never said so but she could sense that Horst knew it. When she was being punished he would have her stand on a stool and lean over the desk so that she was facing the painting. The stool was still there, pushed to the side of the room and stacked with books. It had been retired long ago, not because the punishments stopped, but because the twins outgrew the need for a boost. The painting looked less terrifying then she remembered, but Angie still hadn't outgrown the uneasy feeling it gave her.

It was medieval. In origin, maybe English, but she couldn't be sure. It depicted a bleeding Christ carrying his cross over an inverted trapezoid filled with bright purple clusters of grapes. As he walked a stream of wine mixed with his blood, and the liquid was captured by diminutive workers who poured it into casks. Overhead angels watched the scene with grim faces. Yet it was the image of his blood spilling into the wine that disturbed her the most.

"Did that really happen?" she asked Horst once.

"It's only a painting."

"But was his blood really in the wine? Did they really drink blood?"

"The painting is a metaphor, Angelina."

"But what if blood really did get into the wine? You know, by accident."

Horst thought about this for a moment.

"Nothing would happen. During the fermentation process the yeast would eat it right up."

Angie staggered towards the desk and flipped the switch illuminating *The Blood of Christ.* She could almost feel the warmth from the fireplace on the back of her bare legs. There was always a roaring fire on those nights. Maybe Horst did it to scare them, a Godless man putting the fear of God in them, just a little bit. It wasn't as though he beat them often. Horst reserved his punishments for the big things, like the time Angie pulled out a handful of hair from a migrant worker's daughter's head and had taken a chunk of her scalp with it. Horst was furious. After the incident he sent her to her room without a word. Later that night she was called to the office.

"Angelina."

He kept her waiting in the bedroom for five minutes but it felt like three days. Zach was there of course, and they clung to one another like magnets in the dark of the bedroom. Tilda, the sentinel, was sitting on the bed reading a gossip magazine wearing her best, *that's what you get for being a couple of hellions,* face.

"Angelina, don't make me call you again." Horst never raised his voice in anger. His self-control was purely terrifying. The twins cowered.

With a roll of her eyes, Tilda slid off the bed and separated the two like flypaper from a honeycomb. Holding Zach back by the scruff of the neck, she opened the door with her foot, and shoved Angie in.

Horst stood in the shadows. Looking back on it she was impressed with his theatrics. What a showman. On the desk there was a variety of objects ranging from the minor to the severe: a hairbrush, a shoehorn, a belt, a switch. Her task was to fetch the stool from the wall and choose her instrument of torture. Horst aided her decision with a finely crafted guilt trip.

"Somewhere out there, a little girl is crying herself to sleep tonight with a nice, fist-sized hole torn out of her scalp. Did she deserve this fate?" Dramatic pause. "No. Does anyone?" Sigh. "No. Little Maria doesn't have much. She lives in a shack without fine clothes or toys to play with. She doesn't have video games or a stereo system or even a color TV to watch, nothing to distract her from the pain in her head caused by a girl who she thought was her friend. Is this fair? Is it fair, Angelina?"

"No."

"Good. We agree. Now, if you were in my position, if it was your job to punish the wicked child who did such a horrible thing, which would you use?"

With a trembling hand an eight-year-old Angie reached for the switch. Once her choice had been made she was absolved, and she knew Horst would get the beating over with as quickly and as painlessly as possible. It hurt a little, but her cries were never for herself, they were always out of guilt for what she had done. When it was over he would ask her if she was sorry.

"Yes," she would say through tears, fully meaning it, and he would hug her.

Angie stopped the lump that was rising in her throat. Those punishments were the only times she could remember Horst hugging her. A wave of nausea came over her as she sat, stuck in the muddy trenches of memory lane.

As quickly as she could, she switched off the picture light and forced open the hidden door leading to the roof. She climbed the ladder, and with all her might, threw her shoulder against the trap door. It burst open, revealing blue sky, fluffy clouds and a magnificent view of the whole valley. Angie pulled herself up and took a deep breath of ember-scented air. From this height she could see the source of the fire. They were burning leaves at the Miller's farm.

Still more than a bit shaken, she took a seat in one of two weathered lawn chairs set up on either side of a card table. So this is where Horst and Tilda were, their coffee mugs, their socks. On the table sat two wine glasses coated in purple, one with the trace of lipstick still present, abandoned in the unforgiving sun. The bottle, still half-full, sat on the ground next to Horst's chair. It had become an anthill of epic proportions. There was a newspaper pile between the two chairs and a gossip rag from some months earlier, a pair of reading glasses and a ratty shawl. Again, Angie felt the lump rising, and even let a tear slip past her unsuspecting eyelashes. But she wasn't crying for them and she wasn't crying out of guilt for a migrant child. This time Angie was crying purely for herself.

7 · VITRIOL ·

Kat Slater clicked the mouse on a file marked Lapis and turned her laptop one hundred and eighty degrees to the right.

"Courtesy of the Prosser Development Fund, may I present, the Lapis Estates Hotel and Spa, five star accommodations, all green construction, activities, wine tours, you name it, and we would even leave the main house. It's a landmark, so, you know, it would most likely end up as offices or a gift shop, that kind of thing."

The barn was humming with activity. Gabriel and his crew were stocking the bar with inventory and the event crew had arrived to conduct the tastings. Most of them were old friends of Horst and Tilda and were so torn up over the tragedy that Zach was predicting disaster. He tried to listen to what Kat was saying but kept getting torn away. The only person whose fully rapt attention Kat had captured was Angie's, who stood with her arms folded regarding the computer screen as if it were a benevolent, wish-granting genie.

"Will the spa do back facials? Those things are a godsend, because you never really know what's going on back there."

"Absolutely," Kat beamed.

"I mean, Zack and I are super close but I simply cannot get him to squeeze my blackheads, when they happen, which is rare. But still, I like to be informed."

"The spa will be fully loaded, I can promise you that. And think of all the employment opportunities for the people of Prosser. In this economy…."

"When you're right, you're right."

Zach buzzed by in a tizzy.

"Ladies, can we not do this now?"

"Zach. Zachary," Angie followed him into the barrel room with Kat on her heels.

"I'm busy, this thing starts in twenty minutes. I could use some help, maybe?"

Angie cut her brother off at the pass and wrapped her arms around his neck.

"This is the help," she beamed. "Do you realize what she's offering? It's called the big picture, baby. Give him the numbers again, sweet tits."

Kat swallowed hard and smiled harder.

"Four point eight is what they're offering, but I'm sure I can get five, what with my *sweet tits* and all."

"We're lucky if we pull in five hundred measly bucks tonight, she's offering five million. Zachary…."

Zach separated himself from Angie's grasp.

"Horst would never sell. And you know it."

"Horst is fish food!" Angie exclaimed. A few of the event staffers heard this and excused themselves.

Zach took Angie by the arm and led her back behind a row of barrels.

"Fine Angie, maybe he wasn't father of the year, but he was still our dad and this place is still his legacy. We can't just make a decision like this overnight."

"Why not? What has Lapis been for us but a living hell since Mom died."

"That's a little extreme, Ange."

"Remember Maria? Remember what he did to me? And all those other times? You saw. You were there."

Zach did remember and it made his blood run cold. She could always get him with that one, and she knew it.

"I'm not making any decisions right now. Let's just get through tonight and talk about it tomorrow, okay?"

"Fine. I'm gonna go get wasted now if you don't mind."

"I don't mind, you're a big girl, do what you want."

She leaned in close to him, her breath on his neck in full view of Kat.

"Zachary, darling, I must ask you not to order me around, please."

Zach sighed and stormed off. Angie turned and posed against the barrels.

"Katherine? Would you care for a beverage?"

"Sure."

"Come here first."

Kat knew this game. It was the game every girl at Prosser High School had to play if they wanted to get within ten yards of Zachary Bartlett. It was the Angie game; Kat had played it before. Part of her hoped it would be history, but she knew better then to overestimate Angie. Kat had even tried to reintroduce the Flint factor. With Angie focused on Flint, she would be too ridiculously self-obsessed to give damn what Zach was up to, but it hadn't yet quite worked out the way Kat had planned.

"I want you to kiss me."

"Angie…."

"You know the rules. The more you bitch the worse it'll be."

"We're not in high school anymore. These games don't work."

"Really, Kat? Really? Even when there's a big fat commission on the line? What is five percent of five million anyway? I was always shitty at math."

Kat softened and clipped up close to Angie on her Christian Louboutin heels. She took Angie softly by the wrists and raised her arms above her head, pressing her

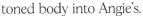

toned body into Angie's.

"Five percent of five million is two-hundred and fifty thousand dollars," she purred, "And I would pay that not to have to kiss you right now, Angelina. So why don't you take your little girl games and try them on someone else. No offence, but you weren't that good."

Angie's mouth dropped open but no words came out. Kat didn't give her a chance to formulate a retort. She turned and left, the stench of Macedonian Vanilla only fueling Angie's rage. Somewhere there was a bottle of Chardonnay with her name on it. In a huff, Angie went to seek it out.

The event was somber but smooth. They practically sold out of their reserve vintage, a Merlot that Horst had taken particular pride in according to Gabriel. It amazed Zachary how many people came out of the woodwork to pay their respects. It was shame Angie was missing it, not that she would care anyway.

Kat was nice enough to lend a hand behind the tasting bar. It seemed the time she put in working for Kestrel, Lapis, and the others, had sharpened her wine knowledge perhaps not to sommelier level, but when it came to the region she could converse with the best of them. It was charming to see her take such an interest, and with her natural powers of attraction, well, a boy could dream. He had to remind himself that at the end of the day she was only there for the money. What they had shared in high school was only ancient history.

"Hey Zach, fancy a break?" Kat asked. Without waiting for an answer she slipped through the kitchen doors. The crowd had begun to thin, and Gabriel seemed to have things under control, so Zach snuck out after her.

He found Kat sitting on the stainless steel countertop in the industrial kitchen Horst had installed earlier that year, smoking a cigarette with her legs crossed. She hadn't bothered to turn on the lights.

"You know, smoking those things will kill your palate."

"Thank you," she exhaled, "for your concern."

Zach gave himself a nervous tour around the new kitchen, opening oven doors and cabinets, the small refrigerators and the factory new walk-in.

He took a roach out of his pocket and fired it up.

"Now this, this is what one might call palate enhancement." He took a hit and passed it to her.

"Why, because it gives you the munchies?" Kat put her cigarette out and played along, taking a deep hit of the roach and handing it back.

"Kind of. Which brings me to my first question, Madame Real Estate Agent, if my father was so eager to sell, why on earth do you think he would go ahead and build this spanking new kitchen?"

"That's easy. Property value."

"Hmm. That almost makes sense, but if I remember correctly, you said that the hotel people were planning on tearing everything down except the house. Isn't that right?"

Kat uncrossed her legs and Zach gravitated closer to her.

"Yes and no. Property value isn't determined by what the new owners plan to do with said property, it's determined at the time of appraisal. By adding the new kitchen, your father made a smart business move. He upped the value of the entire property by several hundred grand."

Zach rested his hands casually on her knees.

"But he spent several hundred to have it put in— and with such attention to detail. If it weren't so dark in here you would notice that these tiles behind you…." He reached past her shoulder and leaned his hand on the wall behind her, pressing his hips between her knees, which spread for him like butter. "These tiles are terra cotta. If I was gonna build a kitchen just to have it demolished, I certainly wouldn't put in terra cotta tiles. It would be a waste on so many levels."

"Maybe your father didn't see it that way."

"And maybe you couldn't get him to sell so you're trying your charms on me."

"Maybe. How am I doing?"

"I don't know, Kat. How are you doing?"

She shimmied her pelvis closer to the edge of the counter and locked her legs around his waist.

"I'm doing just great, thanks."

She kissed him and he kissed back. And it wasn't just any kiss, it was a Kat Slater kiss. His first real kiss in high school, the girl he dreamed about every night, the girl whose picture was pinned up in his locker time and time again, even when Angie took them down. Kat Slater was his could-have-been girl, and now here she was in his arms, in his winery, her lips against his, her hands unbuckling his belt.

He loved her in that moment, and not in the same messy, complicated way he loved Angie. He loved Kat Slater for what she represented, for her confidence and organization. Even her sanity was sexy, her toned, pragmatic sanity. He would have her, right there on the kitchen counter and if he didn't fuck it up, maybe he could get her back. Maybe he could keep her. Angie could return to New York and finish school, do her thing, and he could stay there in Prosser, at Lapis. And Kat could stay with him. It wasn't a commission. It was better. It was a whole life.

Their mouths were locked. Breathing had become a secondary function. *Kat by the locker room. Kat in the school play. Kat touching him on the cafeteria line.* It was all coming back. Maybe this is why he was here. The real reason. It was so long ago. Years since he had been with her. He was her first and he remembered so much about her body. The little things people do, how they do them, and in what order; it's so unique, as unique as fingerprints. His belt for example, the way she pulled too hard at it, her eagerness to hold him in one hand while her other hand wrapped tightly around his neck. He remembered her fondness for exposure and lifted her, pulling her pencil skirt all the way up around her waist. The little sigh as he slipped off her panties was the same little sigh he remembered. Her smell, the feel of her skin, the way it covered her muscles like a layer of satin. He had to physically stop himself from professing his love, but once he pressed inside her, he couldn't help himself, the words just blurted out.

"Oh Jesus, Kat, I love you."

Click.

No.

The light switch. They had been discovered and the look on Kat's face said it all: it was Angie. Zach was afraid to turn around.

"Do you mind?" Kat jumped down from the counter and adjusted her skirt.

"Oh, I mind."

Zach's whole body deflated at the sound of her voice, but he couldn't bring himself to look at her. He was afraid if he did, he might run across the room and throttle her.

"I mind that my brother seems to have developed a taste for whores in his old age."

"How fucking dare you…."

Zach cut Kat off with a wave of his hand. He buckled his pants and turned to face his sister. She was drinking, but that was no excuse. This time she had gone too far.

"Angie, I'm giving you one chance to turn around and leave."

"Then what, Zach? You gonna shoot me with your man gun?"

"I'm not kidding."

He was seriously angry. Angie marveled at how pissy boys got when it came to the gross appendage between their legs. She decided to try a different tactic.

"She insulted me," Angie whined.

"I'm gonna take a wild guess and say that you probably deserved it."

Angie put on her Norma Desmond face and finished off her wine in one gulp.

"Well, isn't this just like old times? What is it Zach? She didn't break your heart completely enough in high school? She didn't rip it out and stomp on it good enough for ya?"

Zach couldn't take anymore. He pushed past both women and rushed out of the kitchen.

Angie yelled after him.

"She wants money! That's the only reason she let you fuck her!

Gabriel, the event staff, and the remaining guests watched surprised as Zach stormed off. Kat pushed past Angie to follow him, but Angie grabbed her by the shoulder, stopping her.

"I'm on to you and there is no way in hell I'm letting you near him."

Kat angrily shook Angie's hand off her arm.

"Just try and stop me," she said.

Without looking back, Kat negotiated her way through the gathered crowd and out into the night. She didn't see Zach anywhere, so she went up to the house and had a quick look around. It was empty and he didn't respond to her calls. She had decided to give up and go home when she heard a familiar sound cut across the valley. Metal on metal—the sliding steel doors of the Lab.

She made her way slowly down the narrow dirt road. It was cold and she was having trouble keeping her footing in the dark on four-inch heels. She was sure Zach was in there. From the path she could see the lights flicker on in their industrial rows. She had to talk to him. She had to at least try and convince him that she wasn't in it just for the money.

"Zach?"

Kat stepped into the huge sterile vat room. The place gave her the creeps, with its high ceilings and giant, stainless steel vats bubbling like futuristic witches cauldrons.

"Zach? I know you're in here."

"Shows how much you know."

Kat looked up. Angie was sitting on the catwalk that gave workers access to the top of the vats, a half empty bottle of white wine in her hand.

"Kestrel's Pure Platinum," she said, holding the bottle up to the light and squinting at it. "My favorite. Know why?"

"Angie, you scared me."

"Because this shit in here," Angie leaned over to slap her hand on the side of a vat, "is just that."

"What?"

"Shit." Angie tipped the bottle back against her lips and giggled.

Kat took a deep breath. "Yeah, well, good night then," she said, turning to go.

"Hey," Angie said loudly, still laughing. She held the Kestrel bottle beside her face so that the label with its image of a leggy blonde was in full view. "I think she even looks like me too. Could be my fucking twin. What do you think?"

Kat glanced back at Angie and hesitated. There was something dangerous in the edge of her voice that was making Kat nervous.

"I think I'm going home."

"Wait Kat, listen to this one," Angie said, suddenly cheerful. "'*Drink wine, and you will sleep well. Sleep, and you will not sin. Avoid sin, and you will be saved. Ergo, drink wine and be saved.*' What do you think of that little play on words, huh? Wanna come get saved with me?" Angie offered the bottle in Kat's direction.

"More games? A minute ago you said I was a whore, now you want to drink with me?"

Angie descended the catwalk steps with a queenly gait.

"I still think you're a whore, Kat. And what's more, you know I'm right. I'm not stupid and neither is my dear sweet brother. His only flaw is the fact that he's male and therefore susceptible to manipulation. You fucked up tonight. You could have gone through me and followed the rules—rules you know all too well—but instead you remade an old enemy. And know this: I still make the decisions for Zach and me. That hasn't changed."

"Are you sure about that?"

"Dead sure." Angie approached her, getting in close. "So much so, that I'm offering you another chance to get it right. We're alone, let's see how good *you* are."

"You're just desperate now."

Kat tried to back away but Angie persisted, cornering her in the space between two of the smaller vats.

"And the better you are, the sooner Zach will be signing on the dotted line."

"This is pathetic."

"Maybe a little."

Angie raised Kat's hands and placed them gently around her neck. Then she slowly sank to her knees.

"Come on, show me what you're made of. You can do it as hard as you want."

"Fuck, Angie, I really don't want to."

"Yes you do. You've wanted to all night."

Kat nearly laughed out loud at the underlying truth in this. Her grip on Angie's slender throat tightened almost automatically.

"Yes. Just do it like I showed you. I'll be good. I won't fight. Then I'll please you. I'll finish what my brother started."

"This is so fucked up. Jesus. If your brother ever found out…then again, Daddy wouldn't mind, but—"

Kat tried a final time to squirm away but Angie had a lock on her and wasn't backing down.

"Kat, stop talking and squeeze…."

CHAPTER EIGHT

8

8 · WINE SPIRIT ·

In Zach's dream it was Kat beside him. It was her hand stroking his face, her warm body pressed up against his. When he awoke to find Angie in his bed his heart sank like a stone. His anger from the previous night came flooding back, but he found it ineffectual, diluted like church wine. It was as if his moment with Kat had been the dream all along and this was his reality. This was his fate. Angelina: the monster in his bed. He was as incapable of separating from her as the head of a coin is from its tail.

Her eyes were open, wide, manic, and she was stroking his face with a dirty, cold hand.

"Oh, good. You're awake." Her breath was rotten and she was still wearing most of her clothes from the previous evening. He wouldn't have been surprised if she hadn't been to bed at all.

"Angie, what…?"

"No Zach. Don't say anything. I need to tell you something."

He flipped over, turning his body away from her and covered his face with a pillow. He groaned.

"I had an amazing idea for the label. Ready? I want to try and recreate Horst's *Blood of Christ* painting. Not all of it, just the bloody feet and the grapes. What do you think?" She wormed her way closer to him and pulled at the pillow. "Are you listening?"

"I'm listening," he moaned.

"Isn't that an amazing idea?"

Yes. It was an *amazing* idea. It wasn't by any means a *good* idea. In fact, it was an amazingly *bad* idea. He couldn't imagine anyone wanting to buy a bottle of wine with such an image pasted to it—let alone all the horrible childhood memories he associated with the damn thing—but it was amazing all right. Amazing that out of all the infinite possibilities in the world, Angie had yet again chosen the most inappropriate image he could possibly conjure.

Something snapped inside of Zach, some distant tree branch in the forest of his mind.

"No. Actually Angie, it's a pretty shitty idea. Who would want to drink a wine with bloody feet on the label? Do you want us to go bankrupt? You may not have liked Horst, but at least he knew the business."

He couldn't look at her. He knew she was probably hurt, and why wouldn't she be? He was being a dick.

"Oh. Well, maybe you're right. That's okay. Dad's office is filled with books and stuff. I'm sure I'll find something that works."

Zach lifted the pillow—Dad? He looked over at the clock. It was 6:17 in the morning.

"Angie, what the hell are you doing up?"

"I got a teensy bit drunk last night, that's all."

She cuddled up next to him and he got a better look at her hands. Her nails were filled with dirt.

"What happened here?"

"Oh Zach, it was so beautiful. I spent the whole night in the vineyard. Like we used to do as kids. I wanted to feel my hands in the soil."

Typical.

"Well, go shower. You're filthy. And brush your teeth while you're at it."

She didn't move.

"Zach?"

"What?"

"Are you mad at me about Kat?"

"A little, yeah."

"Well, I'm sorry."

"It's okay."

She sat up and kissed him.

"I love you."

"Christ, Angie, your breath stinks."

"I love you."

"I love you, too."

She left him and he faded back to sleep. It was only a brief encounter with his sister, one he would later try to convince himself was a dream.

There was work to be done at Lapis that morning and Zach immersed himself in it. He became Gabriel's shadow, relearning much about the art of winemaking that he had forgotten over the years. Gabriel was cordial while taking him through the ropes, but Zach sensed a bit of impatience on the part of his father's old assistant. Zach had a lot of questions and there simply wasn't time for all the answers, not when there were seven vats of wine that needed to be casked. More than once though, Zach had the distinct impression that some of Gabriel's answers were cut intentionally short. He tried to remind himself to be patient. Gabriel was going through a lot of changes in Horst's absence too. They all were.

Later, over lunch, Gabriel mentioned that he had to run some errands in Prosser. There was some shopping that needed to be done and someone needed to stop by Kestrel to pick up a piece of equipment that Horst had arranged to get the week before. Seeing an opportunity to remove himself from Gabriel's hair, Zach quickly offered to do it.

Gabriel rubbed his eyes and ran his hand through

his hair, finally looking at Zach with a wan smile.

"That would be fine, Zachary," he said. "Thank you." He glanced down at his hands and back up at Zach, his smile replaced with a blank expression.

"Perhaps you could take Angelina with you. She is restless too, I think. Perhaps the fresh air would be good. For both of you."

Zach shrugged. If he didn't know better he would swear Gabriel looked relieved at the idea of getting rid of them—maybe even excited? No, that was stupid. Gabriel's face was the same emotionless wall as ever as he furtively checked his watch and excused himself from the lunch table. Zach watched Gabriel hurry off with his own sense of relief. If there were questions Gabriel didn't want to answer, there were also times that Zach felt all too closely watched in the man's presence. It was a prickly feeling, as though there were eyes boring on the back of his skull, and yet when he looked up Gabriel's attention was always elsewhere. Angie would just laugh at him and tell him to get more sleep, of course. Fuck it. Maybe she'd be right for once.

After a sweep of the house, Zach found Angie in their father's office, pouring over books and papers she had scattered on the desk and floor.

"Knock knock," he said leaning in the doorway.

"Go away. Don't want any."

"Not even a ride to town? Take in the sights? Fresh air? Sunlight? Jesus Ange, c'mon. You look like shit in here."

"Thanks but no thanks. Now fuck off Zach. Seriously."

Zach waited but she didn't so much as glance up at him and she didn't look as though she'd taken his shower advice either. Perhaps it was for the best. If she was content to focus on her little art project what business of it was his to stop her? Maybe putting some space between them at the moment would be a good thing anyway. Not to mention the fact that a trip to Kestrel might involve the presence of Flint. And when it came to Flint, Angie was still an unlit match. Bringing the two of them together anymore than necessary could be dangerous.

Zach finally set out alone in his father's favorite pickup truck. He drove slowly past the harvesting workers who stopped what they were doing and removed their hats out of respect for Horst, an unexpected gesture that filled Zach with a somber sense of pride. He got the same reception in town. At the hardware store, the local café, people went out of their way to pay their respects and he found it slightly odd. Horst was a lot of things but Zach never really figured him as the beloved neighbor type. To Zach, Horst had been cold and stern, but to hear the people in town, Horst was a regular George Bailey. Maybe he was only that way to his children.

Zach's last stop was for equipment at Kestrel. It seemed Flint had made a bet with Horst over an antique French basket press and lost. Zach watched while a couple of workers attempted to hoist the broken down old thing into the back of the pickup truck. If he had known that this was the important piece of equipment he was supposed to collect, he might not have bothered.

"She's over a hundred years old, you know." Flint had snuck up behind him. "Your father always loved it."

"Yeah, I can see why."

A chunk of metal fell off the press and hit one of the workers on the side of his leg.

"It must be a winemaker thing."

"Right."

Flint ignored Zachary's sarcasm.

"Hey, come inside for a minute. I want you to check something out."

Zach reluctantly followed. He had always been an ass to Flint. It was just the way things were and they both accepted it as normal.

Inside the familiar tasting room, Flint poured them both some 2005 Co-Fermented Estate Syrah.

"Try it," Flint said with a cool confidence that made Zach roll his eyes.

"Can't. I'm driving,"

"Good thing it's only grape juice."

Zach rolled his eyes again but this time a smile slipped out. He tried the wine.

"Well?"

"Perfume. Lavender. Clove. Then, plum and blackberry. Oak, right?"

"Yes."

"Oh, and mocha."

"Gold star. You're a Thannhauser all right," Flint said using Horst's family name.

"Not really, I'm more of a Bartlett. He told you that story?"

"We saw a lot of each other over the last few years."

"What, he was coming to you for pointers?"

It was well known that in the region Kestrel was the show pony to beat. The student had long surpassed the teacher, and while Horst had his moments, the flame that was Lapis had died down significantly since Eve left the mortal world.

"Quite the opposite, Zachary. Quite the opposite."

"Okay and…?" Damn cryptic winemakers. Just say it already, Zach thought.

"Consider this, you have an exceptionally advanced palate. Let's do a little tasting."

Flint started taking bottles out from under the tasting bar two at a time like a man on a mission. Half of the bottles were from Kestrel, the other half from Lapis, sixteen in all.

"We're gonna taste all those?"

"Yes, um, you may want to spit. Grape juice can catch up with a man."

Flint went into the kitchen and brought out a rack of wine glasses and started pouring.

"There is a point to this, right?"

"Indeed. A mystery if you will. One I've been trying to solve for the past four years. Now, look at this, eight of my wines, eight of your father's. His Chardonnay, my Chardonnay. Same year, '05. Try them. Tell me what you get."

Zach tasted them both.

"Yours is better."

"Without a doubt. I encouraged malolactic fermentation. Horst left it out. An odd choice, and inferior grapes. He doesn't hand sort. So…."

"So what's your point?"

"Next one. Cabernet."

Zach tasted.

"Kestrel wins again."

"Why?"

"I don't…?"

"Old barrels. And something slightly less quality about the grapes, right? I don't think he was punching down the cake enough. Do you know if he uses a must pump?"

"I don't know, Flint. What's the fuckin' point? You know I wasn't crazy about my old man, but you don't need to insult his work to my face so soon after he—"

Flint poured out two more glasses.

"Here. This is the mystery. Just one more, okay? My '05 Merlot."

Zach downed the whole glass in one gulp.

"Okay, got that? Now, Horst's."

Flint handed the glass to Zach as if it were the Holy Grail. He tasted it.

There it was again. The knee-weakening feeling

he had the night he arrived in the Lab with Gabriel. It was something about the Merlots. Some unquantifiable element that was less of a flavor and more of a feeling. The other night it had been fresh, like a first kiss. But this one, the '05, was almost painful. The emotion was love to be sure, but a sad, longing kind of love. One that had lived many years longer than him. The closest word that made sense was earth, but not earth in a stagnant form the way he usually pictured it. This earth was alive, and feeling, and moving, and longing—for a seed perhaps.

Flint's eyes were wide. He was waiting for a big reaction and Zach didn't plan on giving him one.

"I guess Horst wins that hand. I gotta go. My sister's all alone at the house."

Zach left the tasting room and crossed the lot back to the pickup. Flint hurried to keep up.

"How does he do it, Zach? Please tell me he told you before he died."

Zach kept walking.

"I mean, at first I thought it was a reserve batch, one he was just really precious about. But there's something else. Some element I just—I don't know."

"I don't know either, Flint. And even if I did, do you really think I'd tell you?"

"You might for the right price."

"You're offering me money?" The clunky French press had been tied into the back of the pickup with hemp rope. "Or maybe another antique piece of crap?"

"I'll teach you everything. Everything I know."

Zach stopped walking and Flint gave him a serious look.

"You have a gift for this, Zach, but bringing Lapis back up to where it needs to be will take the kind of knowledge that Gabriel doesn't have."

"And if I don't know how he did it?"

"Very few secrets die completely, you just have to look for the clues."

"Yeah, well, Angie and I are going back to New York in a few days so I guess you're shit outta luck."

Now it was Flint's turn to be sarcastic.

"Oh right, I heard you guys have quite the promising music career. Good luck with that."

Zach got in the pickup and started the engine. He slammed the door in front of Flint who stepped back and tipped his hat.

"Call me if you change your mind," he said.

CHAPTER 9

NINE

9 · BOIL ·

In Horst's office time passed without anything to mark it, only the quiet flames in the fireplace and the low lamplight reflecting off the glass bookshelves. Morning turned to day and then late afternoon as Angie sat unaware, her body slouched over the desk, straightening only occasionally to turn a page or throw another book onto the pile at her feet. She was sleep deprived and dirty, and though she hadn't quite planned to scavenge through every last scrap of paper in the office, once she had started looking it seemed impossible to stop.

First there was the books themselves, a vast library of tomes on alchemy, theology, history, and art. The old man's obsessions entombed and displayed behind the glass with their gilt-edged spines, the odd note scrawled and stuck haphazardly between their pages. Paper musings that made no sense to her, pressed flat and forgotten over the years.

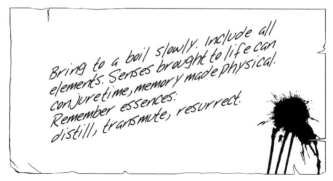

Bring to a boil slowly. Include all elements. Senses brought to life can conjure time, memory made physical. Remember essences: distill, transmute, resurrect.

Sometimes she paused and stared at the fire without seeing it exactly. It occurred to her in those moments that her father had been a man afflicted by profound sadness. What other explanation was there for such a long and full life that was reduced to *this* in the end? An office that was like a beautiful coffin, filled with notes that only ever had meaning for their originator, the weight of Horst's knowledge contained in a sealed cube without any windows to the outside world. Just like his life, hidden behind a closed door, Angie thought. It was a depressing thought, and for a moment she almost felt for the man. Not that she forgave him. She did not. It was his duty as a parent to put the emotional welfare of his children first, and he had utterly failed them in that respect.

These were thoughts that did not end. They just went round and round in her mind like a record stuck on a groove. Pity, anger, rinse and repeat. Angie opened and shut books mechanically, pausing only when a postcard slid out from one of the books and into her lap. *The Blood of Christ.* The image was grainy and darker than the original hanging on the wall overhead, but she was still transfixed by the blood flowing into wine, the angels' serene white faces. She turned the postcard over but found it blank, a small gold key taped simply in the center. Instinctively she tore the key loose and tried it on the locked drawer at the bottom of Horst's desk. She wasn't surprised when it turned easily and the catch released as though it had been waiting for just that moment.

The drawer was mostly empty. A few tattered notebooks, a manila envelope stuffed with ledgers, and beneath them a small square metal box. She half-expected it to be locked as well, but it swung open easily. Inside were stacks of letters tied in ribbons, ink sketches of vines heavy with grapes, and of course, the photographs. They *did* exist then, and when she thought about it, they were just what she had been hoping to find.

Horst, Eve, her mother, her father. They were there, suddenly, rising from the shadows in one brilliant instant. Angie felt as though she had been punched in her gut and her fingers trembled slightly as she plucked a faded picture from the stack. It was Horst in cream-colored linen and a Panama hat—a cliché and ridiculous costume even for a winemaker—his smile barely giving away the fact that he was in on the joke. Eve stood beside him in a long frontier skirt and a gossamer thin camisole, braless, with a wide brimmed hat and pruning sheers hanging like weapons of valor from her belt. She was radiant, and standing in her light Horst glowed as well, a completely different person than the dark father figure Angie remembered. She flipped through the snapshots slowly, committing each one to memory. Each picture was another image of her parents posing together, some part of their bodies always in contact with the other, almost always with a vineyard at their backs. In some of the pictures the twins were in the background like little cherubs adorning the romantic image of love.

Angie returned the photographs to the box and untied a bundle of letters, unfolding the top one carefully with the palm of her hand. The writing was familiar but it wasn't and suddenly Angie could almost hear her mother's voice whispering the words in her ear:

Dearest Horst,

I have been in the vineyard all day. The house was too stuffy and I couldn't seem to get enough air into my lungs. Each breath was like a gasp.

The children and I stomped the grapes with our bare feet. They had a marvelous time. An hour of pure laughter, pure joy, and I think it will become a fine memory for them. The physical essence of a thing, no matter how brief, cannot be destroyed, only transformed. Remember? You showed me that.

Now I am alone. The cake is still warm, drying on my legs, and every cell in my body cries out for it to consume me the way it has consumed us countless times before. This is no less true than it ever was. You may be afraid, but please know that I am not. Can you see? It is inescapable, this destiny.

Even when I am gone I will still be with you.

Yours eternally,
~E

Angie read the letter four times before refolding it and placing it back with the others. In the end Horst was just the man who barely raised her, a shadow presence slipping in and out of her life over the years. His stern face and the way he had spoken of his—*their* life—as though it were only divided into a before and after. Before, was life with their mother, his Eve. And after, the *now* he always insisted on so strongly, was the only thing that mattered. *She got very sick and died*, was all he would say of Eve in the years that came after. And when the twins grew older and started fishing for details, they were met with his chilly anger and excuses. After he and Tilda married, Horst flat-out refused to discuss Eve at all. As if she had never existed. Of all the things her father may or may not have been, this was the one thing Angie found she could not forgive him for.

Angie sighed and slid back in the leather chair. She closed her eyes and pressed her fists into her temples, massaging them gently. It was how she always tried to reconcile her thoughts of Eve, a woman she only remembered in the broadest of strokes, the bonds of motherhood merely a technicality. The only specifics Angie remembered popped up like a slideshow of stills in her mind. Eve holding Zach by the waist, smiling, their cheeks pressed together. Angie and Zach balanced one on each side of Eve's lap, toddlers then and barely aware of the world around them. Mostly though Angie remembered running wild through the vines with Zach behind her, flashes of her mother staring fixated at Horst, oblivious to their childish behavior. And maybe that was okay, Angie thought. Why should children consume the lives of their parents?

The room was warm from the fire and Angie felt flushed suddenly, dizzy. She opened her eyes to focus on the stacks of papers and books littering the desk in front of her. She had the sudden urge to destroy everything, to feed the fire and watch it all burn. It was all lies anyway, lies of the dead haunting the living. She didn't want to know any more. With a violent sweep of her arms, Angie rose and cleared the surface of the desk to the floor. Fuck them all. What she wanted was to get the hell out of Prosser before it dragged her down into its depths. Angie sank back into the chair with her head in her hands.

"Angelina."

Angie jumped at the sound of her name, spoken softly but sharply. Gabriel stood in the doorway with his hands folded in front of him. The glow of the fire lit up the right side of his face, casting the left in a deep shadow so it looked as though he was wearing half a mask. He stepped closer and glanced mildly at the jumble of papers and books strewn across the room. His gaze took in the metal box lying at the foot of the desk and he smiled stiffly.

"You have been busy I see."

Angie stiffened in her seat. "I have a right to be here," she said coolly. "And you could learn how to knock."

"Of course. My apologies, Angelina. Dinner is waiting for you in the kitchen, should you want it." Gabriel turned to leave the room.

"Wait."

Gabriel stopped with his hand on the doorknob.

"How did she die?" Angie asked.

She paused then sprung from her chair, grabbing the metal box from the floor to thrust it in his direction. "You were there, Gabriel. Tell me. Please."

Gabriel turned around. He looked at her steadily and nodded his head.

"Tell me what all this means," she gestured with her arms at the office around them and placed the metal box on the desk. She sank back into the leather chair, suddenly exhausted. "What it was he kept from us. You could do that. I know you could."

Gabriel sat down in an empty chair to the side of the desk and took a pair of reading glasses from his front pocket. He put them on and picked up the letter Angie had read, examining it briefly before folding it and returning it to the box.

"No."

"What do you mean, no?"

"I mean, I don't know. Your father, he worked very hard. He always did. She wrote him many letters, even when they were in the same room together she wrote him letters. And he kept them it seems, every one."

"Why was she unhappy?"

Gabriel looked frustrated. "She wasn't. It was the beginning of her illness and they knew. They always knew."

"They knew what? She said she couldn't breathe. Was it her lungs? Was it cancer?"

"Cancer, yes." Gabriel kept his eyes on hers without blinking and she knew he was lying. Why was he lying?

"Lung cancer? And she died in the hospital? Chemo, the whole nasty business? I don't remember any of that."

"You wouldn't, Angelina. It was a long time ago and you were very young."

He was avoiding her gaze so Angie placed her hands over his.

"You're lying to me," she said.

Gabriel paused. He took in her dirty and scratched hands, the bruises just beginning to blossom at the sides of her neck. He shook off her hands and rose from his seat.

"It is not my place to question things, Angelina. The past is the past."

Angie jumped up, startling them both.

"Gabriel, fucking talk to me!" she screamed.

Gabriel grabbed a handful of papers from the floor and held them out to her.

"There is nothing here! These books and papers," he shouted, throwing the papers in the fire, "they are nothing! You want to find the Enóloga, look in the fields. In the vineyard he loved, not in this tomb."

Gabriel took a minute to compose himself, then bowed slightly at the waist, straightening to back out of the room without another word.

Angie let him go. She *was* tired after all, too tired for a fight. It was the room. She needed air.

She rose and climbed the ladder to the widow's walk two rungs at a time. On the roof the sky was washed with color, a violent sunset in tangerine, persimmon, and blood orange, their colors splashed across the horizon like a wound. Angie took it in all at once, the great expanse of it, and drew in a breath so deep she thought the reverse might be true. That it might, just might, be possible to drown in an excess of air. She stood where she was on the highest spot of Lapis thinking about what Gabriel had said as the last bit of day slid into night. Out there was the Horst he had known and she envied him that. Angie stood there without moving, not even as she watched the police car wind its way closer, its blue lights flashing soundlessly over the fields. Only when she saw the sheriff park in front of the Lab did she turn and go inside.

CHAPTER TEN

10

10 · ROT ·

Kat Slater had fans in Prosser. She wasn't the kind of girl the town could do without for very long, so when she failed to show up at work the day after the Lapis tasting event, calls were made. It started easily enough when a lovesick coworker decided to swing by Kat's apartment to see if she was alright. She wasn't answering her phone, which was very out of character for the firm's top realtor who was known for her nearly incestuous relationship with her cell phone. And later, after returning to the office empty handed, that same coworker put in a call to the sheriff's department. Kat wasn't answering her door and her coworker was afraid that something might be wrong, a suspicion that grew when he checked the garage and found her car missing.

Sheriff Jim Griffith knew Kat. She had gone to school with his daughter. From what he could remember she was a nice enough girl, if not a bit too mature for her age. His immediate thought was that she had taken the day off. Maybe went over to Kennewick to do some shopping. The guy on the phone sounded worried, but Jim assured him he had seen this kind of thing before.

"Sometimes people just need a change of air," Jim said in a tone that was far less comforting then it was patronizing. "She'll turn up."

Normal protocol was to give these kinds of things twenty-four hours. Jim took the kid's name, Brad Hemmings—he remembered that name too, Brad was the skinny, limp wristed kid who acted in his daughter's drama club—filed a quick report, shaking his head and grinning the whole time, and went to track down a late lunch.

After carefully considering his options, Jim drove his patrol car over to Becky's Café for a cup of coffee and a sandwich. He ordered a fat-free hazelnut latte and a buffalo mozzarella panini with sun-dried tomatoes and a pesto aioli. He got a nice table by the window with a view of the street and was about to dig in when his cell phone rang. He put the greasy panini down and wiped his hands on his pants, flipping his phone open just in the nick of time.

"Griffith."

"Hi Jim," his deputy chirped.

"What is it, Grace?" Jim did his best to negotiate the sandwich with one hand, losing a chunk of mozzarella in the process. "I'm kind of busy here."

"Oh, okay, well, I just got another call from the Coldcrest Realty people, they're really freakin' out over there. I was thinking I'd just pass by and see what all the hullabaloo is about."

Jim had a mouthful of panini.

"Hullabaloo? There is no hullabaloo. She's probably in…," he swallowed, "She's probably just gone over to Kennewick or something."

"But she didn't come home last night."

Jim put the sandwich down with a grumble.

"How do you know that?"

"Her boxer, Yves. They say he's been locked in the house all night. He's crying and barking, and Brad said she would never just leave Yves like that."

"Alright," Jim said, "I'll take a ride over there if it makes everybody happy."

Jim finished his lunch, thanked Becky, and headed out to Coldcrest Realty. When he got there the receptionist led him past the potted rubber plants and back to the grey fluorescent-

✦

lit office where he found Brad with Yves squirming in his lap.

"Sheriff, finally." Brad was beside himself.

"Where'd the dog come from?" The little boxer puppy hopped down and started jumping up on Jim's legs.

"I got her landlord to let me in. Something's not right, and I'm thirty-percent psychic on my mother's side, so I should know."

Pamela, a pretty senior realtor who sold Jim his vacation cabin, took Brad's side.

"It is really strange, Jim. She loves that dog like it's a baby or something. She would never just leave him."

All eyes were on the reluctant sheriff and while he wanted to tell them not to worry, to reiterate that this kind of thing was not unusual and that Kat would probably turn up all on her own, he felt pressed to do something, anything, if only to prove to them that their tax dollars were not being spent in vain. Sure it would waste a perfectly good afternoon, but it looked as though the citizens of Prosser needed him. Jim sighed.

"Okay then, when was the last time you saw her?"

The question prompted six different accounts of the previous evening, all of them coming to the same anticlimactic conclusion. Kat had left the office early to show a property then she was planning a stop at Lapis for the Fall Crush event. Jim listened to each realtor carefully, even taking notes, and when they were done yapping, he answered their wide-eyed stares with a brilliantly crafted piece of detective work posed as a simple question.

"Does anyone know which property she was showing?"

Pamela led the Sheriff to Kat's desk adorned with photos of her recent trip to Paris, Yves, and several large portraits of herself in a variety of glamorous poses. Tucked in the corner of one of the frames was a snapshot of her and Zachary Bartlett in their formal wear on the way to the junior prom. Feeling his detective juices beginning to flow, Jim plucked the snapshot from the frame and sat down at Kat's desk. After staring at the image for a moment he put the picture in his pocket and began to go through Kat's day planner.

"Here. October twelfth. Looks like she was showing a house out on Wine Country Road. 1232. I can check it out." Sheriff Jim leaned back in Kat's chair and crossed his arms. "You know, it seems to me like you people really take chances out there."

"Sheriff?" Pamela, Brad and the crew listened intently.

"Well, you drive out to these empty houses and meet with total strangers, you never can tell what kind of folks are gonna show up. It's risky."

Six pairs of eyes widened.

"Now, I'm gonna drive out there and have a look-see. As I said, it's probably nothing. If Miss Slater hasn't shown her pretty face by tomorrow, I'll put out a bulletin. One of you gonna look after that dog?"

Sheriff Jim left Coldcrest Realty puffed up like a pigeon. The air on the street tasted different that afternoon. It tasted something like danger, and for the first time in a while, Jim felt like an officer of the law.

He drove out to Wine Country Road and met with the Nathaniels, the nice family still occupying the pretty little Craftsman at number 1232. Not the picture of fearsome desolation he was expecting, but he did manage to collect some information, another cup of coffee, and a slice of cherry pie. Kat Slater had shown the house the previous evening, and, as a matter of fact, the Nathaniels had seen her again later that night at Lapis for the Fall Crush. She was conducting the tasting with Zachary Bartlett. And the Nathaniels didn't like to gossip, but they felt it necessary to mention that there had been a bit of a scene involving Kat, Zachary, and his twin sister Angelina.

Now that name Jim knew all too well. Angelina Bartlett. That girl had been a source of constant strife for his daughter Samantha all through high school. Angelina Bartlett was a bully. Five foot three with the temperament of an angry raccoon. Jim had tried talking to the parents, the father and stepmother, but they were, well, *odd* was the only word for it.

Did he know that the elder Bartletts had passed on recently in a plane crash? Jim had heard something of that nature. That was probably the reason for all the tension, the couple continued. The children were almost certainly stricken with grief. First their mother, now this.

"Their mother?" Jim asked casually, stretching back in his chair. A story was starting to take shape in his mind but the details were still fuzzy.

"Eve, was it? What happened to her now again?"

Mrs. Nathaniel offered the sheriff another slice of pie. He accepted and they kindly filled him in on what details they knew of the Bartlett family. Sheriff Griffith took notes dutifully and asked questions, all the time half-waiting for his phone to ring. But as the story came back to him and the afternoon waned, the little knot in his stomach he called instinct—the one that had led him to join the force in the first place—stopped waiting for the call from Grace telling him that Kat had turned up. His gut knew it wasn't coming.

By the time Jim got back in his patrol car and started heading up towards Hinzerling Road, the sun had settled on the horizon cutting earth and sky in two with a giant red-orange banner.

"*Red skies at night, a vintner's delight,*" Jim sang to himself as he drove, "*Red skies at dawn, vintners be warned...."* He hesitated a moment before speeding up, flicking his blue lights on at the same time. No use wasting those tax dollars if that was what they were there for after all.

Zach was in the Lab. He had been there all afternoon doing a bit of his own research into the mystery Flint had presented. Zach was so wrapped up in his work, that he didn't notice the uneasy looks some of the workers were giving him. His brain had practically fermented. When the patrol car pulled up outside the Lab, it took Gerardo a second to snap him out of his yeasty haze.

"Enóloga, la policía está aquí."

"Police?"

Zach put down what he was doing and met Sheriff Griffith at the door. It had been years since he'd seen the kindly constable, known around town for being something of an easy target. Angie joked that all the members of the Griffith family resembled, in their own way, millionaire Donald Trump. Just seeing the sheriff, his wife, or their daughter would send her into a fit of the giggles. It was mean, childish, and frighteningly accurate. "Sheriff Griffith, hi." Zachary wiped his hands on his jeans. "What brings you out here?"

"I'm on unofficial business. May I speak with you for a minute?"

Zach assumed the visit had something to do with Horst. Maybe the local authorities had some more information on the crash, though in retrospect he couldn't see how. Jim took his hat in his hands as Zach led them inside.

"How's the harvest going?"

Jim showed himself around the vat room provoking cool looks from Gerardo who stayed close as a watchdog.

"Not bad. I guess I kinda got thrown into things around here. I'm just trying to figure it all out."

"Yes, I heard about your parents. My condolences."

"Thank you."

"How long have you and your sister been in town?"

"We just got in the night before last."

Jim put his hand against one of the vats.

"It's warm."

"Yeah, the grapes generate heat when they ferment."

There was an awkward pause as the sheriff ran his hand along the side of the vat.

"So, what's the unofficial business?"

"Kat Slater's gone missing."

Zach's heart dropped into his stomach. A series of images flashed across his cerebral cortex starting with the night before and ending with Angie in his bed that morning. Within split seconds, his mind started organizing those images into horrific scenarios that he deleted as soon as they began to take shape.

"Kat?"

"She didn't show up to work this morning and the folks at her office were worried."

That was a slight relief. They were drinking. She was probably just at home sleeping off her hangover. He tried to come up with a way to explain this to Sheriff Griffith without incriminating her for drunk driving.

"I gave her some wine to take home with her, she probably—you know—she might have had a late night."

"She never made it home, Zach."

Zach had begun to sweat and he was sure that Sheriff Griffith noticed. Angie's dirty hands took center stage in his mind's eye. What had she done?

"Look Sheriff, I hadn't seen Kat in years before last night. She was here, but she left. It must have been around ten."

She probably had a boyfriend that she went to see, or a friend, or maybe she was stranded somewhere with a

flat tire, Zach thought. There had to be an explanation.

"God, I hope she's okay," said Zach.

"Did she do or say anything last night that might help us to locate her?"

"No…."

"No?"

Zach remembered that after the fight with Angie he had gone for a walk in the vineyard to clear his head. When he went back to the barn, both Angie and Kat were gone.

"I—no."

"But there was an argument? Some of your guests mentioned that your sister and Miss Slater, well, that there was some yelling involved?"

"That? That was nothing. Dumb high school stuff. Angie and Kat never really got along." Zach realized he was digging a hole. He had to get out of there as cleanly as possible and talk to Angie. "Look, sheriff, Kat Slater's an amazing person, in fact she was doing some work for my father before he died, that's why she was up here. She was going over some of his plans for Lapis. I just—if there is anything I can do to help, I will. I mean, I know she'll turn up, but if there's anything at all…."

Zach exhaled. He must have looked guilty, but of what? Where was the sheriff going with all of this?

"Is Angelina at home?"

"She's up at the house going through our father's records. I can get her if you want."

Jim smiled.

"No, it's okay, Zachary. You kids have enough to deal with right now. But do me a favor, if you think of anything else, or if you hear from Kat, just call the station, okay?"

"Yeah. Absolutely."

Jim was convinced the kid was telling the truth; he was obviously too terrified to lie. Besides, it was a little unfair of him to be grilling Zach in this way. Kat wasn't even officially missing yet. He dialed back the interrogation a couple of notches.

"You're not in trouble, okay?"

"Okay," Zach forced a deep breath, "what now?"

"If we don't hear from her by tomorrow, I'll put out an APB on her car and we'll go from there. If we can find the car, we'll find the girl."

"Oh, okay. She drives a black BMW. I think."

"Why don't you get some rest?"

"Okay."

Zach was in a haze. He escorted Sheriff Griffith to his patrol car and stood there frozen until his taillights had long disappeared around the first bend in Lapis drive. Zach felt like a deer caught in the path of an oncoming car and he didn't know which way to run. Gerardo snapped him out of it with a tap on the shoulder.

"Enóloga."

Enóloga was his father's nickname, the Spanish word for winemaker. Horst had insisted on it for years, preferring it to *Horse*, which is how his name inevitably sounded on the Spanish tongue. The workers had bestowed the title on Zach since his return, and he hadn't thought to correct them.

"Tengo que mostrarte algo," Gerardo continued, motioning Zach in the direction of the door.

Zach followed Gerardo up to the barn on foot. The night was cool and clear, and the rising moon was bright, casting an eerie silver glow over the vines. Zach knew it was ridiculous, but he couldn't help but feel a tiny bit relieved with every row he passed, grateful that they were just as long, and straight, and empty as he expected them to be.

They reached the barn and Gerardo led him around the side. On busy nights they would use that relatively hidden area for extra parking. At the end of the empty row, a black BMW sat parked in the moonlight like an apparition.

✛

"We thought she was with you," Gerardo said. The young worker stepped back, giving Zachary room to process what he was seeing.

Zach went to the car and looked inside to verify the worst. Hanging from the rearview mirror was an air freshener shaped like a boxer puppy and on the passenger seat were a bunch of papers printed with the Coldcrest Realty logo.

"Fuck, fuck. Who else knows about this?"

"Manuel, Carlos, Rudy."

"Does Gabriel know?"

"I don't think so."

"Get Gabriel. Tell him to meet me up at the house, now."

Gerardo took off back towards the Lab and Zach ran to the house, hardly breathing, hardly thinking, his mind fixed on his destination.

He found her in bed.

"Angie. Angie, wake up."

Zach flipped on the garish overhead light and Angie groaned.

"Dude, I'm trying to sleep."

"Well, get up. What did you do to Kat?"

"God."

"Ange, seriously. Sheriff Griffith was just here."

She peeked out from under her pillow.

"Griffith? You mean, *The Donald*? She called *The Donald* on me? She is so fired." Angie pulled the pillow back over her eyes and giggled. "Besides, I already saw him. Racing over to catch all those drunk drivers I suppose. Tell him to come back later, would ya?"

"What did you do, Ange?" Zach was yelling now and Angie was getting irritated. She sat up and flipped her hair over her shoulder, the tips still damp from a recent shower.

"Nothing. Jesus! Do you realize that you become a total dick when it comes to that girl?"

"She's missing, Ange. And her car is parked behind our barn."

"Missing? What the hell are you talking about?"

"Just tell me what happened last night."

"We talked, that's all."

Zach noticed the bruises on her neck.

"Oh God, Ange. You didn't, did you?"

"We were drunk," Angie sighed. "Maybe I messed with her a little bit but she wasn't having any of it. She gave me this and then she left." Angie traced the bruises with her finger. "Cold fucking fish if you ask me."

"You're amazing."

"Thank you."

"You couldn't just leave it alone, could you? God forbid I have one minute of happiness…."

"Oh please, with that slut?"

Zach saw red. He grabbed Angie by the hair and pinned her to the bed, smacking her head against the headboard as she went down. She yelped.

"Take that back."

"No!"

He shook her by the shoulders, her back arching into him, her toes curling. She loved his anger and he knew it, but he couldn't help himself.

"I said take it back!"

"You idiot," she laughed, "You fucking sap. You think she loves you? You think she even likes you? You may not be able to, but I can see that girl for what she is, an opportunistic whore!"

Zach released her and stood up like a shot.

"Fine! You can deal with your own shit from now on, Angie. I'm through protecting you."

Angie tossed her hair and smiled sweetly.

"No you aren't Zach. You'll always protect me, and I'll

always protect you. That's just the way it is, so get fucking used to it."

He stormed out of her room, slamming the door behind him. What a psycho. What an infuriating, maddening, psycho. For a moment he wished it was Angie who had gone missing. Or even better that he was the one. That would be the only way to get away from her. Just vanish in the night.

When he got downstairs, Gabriel was in the kitchen with Manuel, Carlos, Rudy, and Gerardo. All five men stood silently, waiting for him. They had probably heard everything. Some boss he was turning out to be.

Gabriel stepped forward and paused as if he were about to make a speech.

"Zachary, when your father was alive, all of us, we— let's just say, we took our loyalty to him very seriously. Now that he is gone, you are the Enóloga and our loyalty is with you. If something needs to be done, anything, you can count on us to do it. Do you understand?"

Zach sat at the table and put his head in his hands.

"Yes, thank you," he mumbled.

"So for example," Gabriel continued, "if there were a car out there that might be better off somewhere else, it could be moved. For you. Is that something you would be interested in?"

"Yeah. Yes?"

"Okay then. Consider it done. Goodnight, Enóloga."

The cryptic caravan left and Zach poured himself a giant glass of Horst's Merlot. He caught his own reflection in the wine glass as he brought it away from his lips. He looked tired, older, distorted, and once again, not like himself. For a moment it was his father's face that stared back at him, and for the first time Zach could remember, Horst seemed pleased.

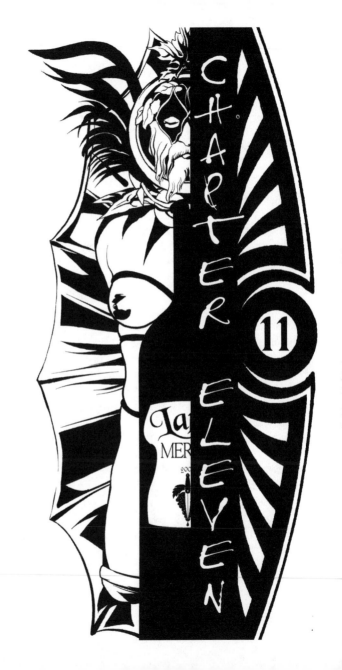

CHAPTER ELEVEN

11

11 · FILTER ·

When they were young, the twins collected mutations. If the anatomy of an acorn was corrupted, if it had two rounded bulbs and only one cap, it would go in a bag or inside a pocket along with the five-leafed clovers, legless lizards, misshapen leaves, and even once, a tiny two-headed snail. Though fully separated from one another, the twins felt an affinity for all things conjoined, for the slightly askew, for the poetry of a soul knit so tightly to another soul that it refused to let go. They saw such anomalies of nature as fortunate, even ambitious, as if the conjoined thing in question was trying to cheat evolution, or at least suggest another alternative. Such creatures would go forth together, hand in hand, hip against hip, and never be alone for they knew best that there is safety in numbers.

Zach was afflicted with dark thoughts all night and his musings, along with a bottle of enchanted Merlot, led him to his father's office. He had to prove the little voice inside his head wrong. There was no way Angie could have hurt Kat, because if she was capable of something that horrible, then so was he. They were the same. He spent the night brooding in his father's leather chair with a wine glass in hand, and that's how Angie found him the next morning, where he had finally curled up to sleep like a puppy under the mahogany desk.

She wanted to curl up beside him. The gravitational pull towards her brother was the strongest force in her life, but she resisted and opted to watch him sleep. He had been so angry with her the night before and she had gotten little sleep thinking about him. Was it possible to lose Zach, really lose him, over this, over anything? Maybe he was starting to pull away from her. Again it dawned on Angie that their closeness might have a shelf life, that at some point Zach might not want her around anymore. And if that day came, could she go on? Would she want to?

Cynics and atheists say that we come into this world alone and that we die alone, and the time in between is nothing but a series of doomed attempts to undermine this inevitability, and like them, Angie liked to think she was not afflicted by thoughts of either religion or self-deception. But twins don't enter the world alone, she thought. She leaned in closer so she was almost touching her brother's hair. Their souls were like the mutated acorn, separate, but wearing one cap.

She sat on the floor beside him while he slept, stroking the air above his head with her fingertips, her head resting on the seat of her father's chair. The room looked strange from that angle. She could see the underside of Horst's desk where there seemed to be an odd buckling in the wood. She leaned over to touch it but it wasn't wood. There was something taped to the bottom of the desk, an old manila envelope. She pulled it free, opened it, and let the contents spill onto the rug.

They were snapshots of women, naked and exposed.

"Oh you kinky bastard."

From what Angie could gather she was looking at twelve different women, one in each photograph. The setting was the same for each: a twilight vineyard, a row of plants intertwined horizontally across the frame with

a gap in the center where a much different vine was growing. Angie held one of the pictures up to the light. The woman was planted in the dirt up to her ankles, her face covered in an elaborate mask. She was naked, arms spread wide, with her hands shadowed in the grapes and foliage at either side of her body. To complete the picture, she was bound to the vine with trellis wire in a brutal display of sadism. Angie flipped through the eleven other photographs. Each one was composed in the same style, only the body shapes and sizes of the women varied slightly. She flipped them over again and studied each one carefully before alerting her brother.

"Holy shit, Zach." Angie shook him by the shoulder, waking him.

Zach turned over groggily and saw Angie sitting cross-legged on the floor. In her black dress, with her two-tone mane pulled back into a long ponytail and her lips painted blood red, she looked like a Gothic doll, pale and perfect. Zach was overcome with remorse. He lurched over on his stomach and pulled himself into the lap of his cruel mistress—his heroin, his arm, his foot, his acorn—and buried his face in the folds of her skirt.

"I'm sorry, Angel. Don't hate me."

"Angel?" He hadn't called her that in years. She nuzzled the back of his neck with her nose and lips for a moment before pulling away from him. There was no time for reconciliation.

"I forgive you. Now look at these."

Zach propped himself up on his elbows and peered at the pictures Angie had spread out on the floor.

"What the hell…? Who are they?"

"They're wearing masks."

"Where did you get these?"

Angie showed Zach the envelope.

"It was taped up here."

"My God."

"That filthy old pervert." Angie couldn't help but smile. "Well at least this proves we're not adopted."

"You think Horst took these himself?"

"Who else could have done it?"

"I don't know. It could be niche porn. Maybe he hired a photographer to take them."

Even as the words left his lips Zach knew it was wishful thinking. This was no doubt his father's handiwork. As disturbing as it was, it fit the modus operandi of the man he knew, though it also gave Zach a more complete picture of his father then he ever wanted to have.

Angie attempted to arrange the photographs into some kind of numerical order. For her they provided validation of a different kind.

"Oh come on, Zach."

As Zach leafed through the pictures, he thought of what Flint had said the day before. All that crap about clues and secrets that never die. Zach almost smiled in spite of himself. Wait until he had a chance to tell Flint what they had indeed uncovered. Not a secret winemaking technique, but a father's guilty fetish.

"Yeah, well, Get rid of them. We have work to do."

Angie had no intention of doing any such thing. There was something to the pictures that she couldn't quite put her finger on yet, but for Zach's sake she gathered them up and put them back in the envelope.

"What kind of work?"

"We need to find Kat."

"Oh, that." Angie flopped backwards onto the floor and started turning the envelope over and over in her hands. "She'll surface when she's done with her little tantrum."

"You wanna tell that to the police?"

"Sure. We're innocent right?"

Zach got up and began to pace back and forth in front of the fireplace.

"We *are* innocent, aren't we Zach?"

"Yes, but I had Gabriel…well, I had him relocate her car."

"You did what? Why?"

Angie could feel the Jesus in *The Blood of Christ* painting watching them with disapproving eyes.

"Just in case."

"Just in case what, Zach? Just in case I killed her and buried her body in the vineyard?"

"I was protecting you. Like you wanted."

"Well fuck, Zach." Angie stood and blocked his way to stop him from pacing. "That is the sweetest thing you've ever done for me."

Zach shrugged her off.

"No, think about it. Part of you thought I actually went and killed the bitch, and despite your feelings for her, you covered my tracks anyway. Oh Zach, I always knew I could count on you to commit perjury for me." She danced in front of him, mocking him with her smile.

"I'm a model brother."

"You're a prince," Angie said, throwing her arms around his neck, "and I worship you."

"Then help me find Kat," Zach said. He untangled Angie's arms from around his neck and started towards the door.

Angie didn't move. Instead she leaned against the desk with all the sass of a crooked detective's mol.

"Hermano, I don't want to spoil your wild goose chase but if you wanna find *tight-abs* then I suggest you start looking right here."

"And where exactly is *here*?"

She picked up the manila envelope from were she had dropped it and pulled out the first picture on the pile.

"You mean you didn't notice?" She handed it to Zach with a dramatic flick of her wrist. "I told you she was a whore."

"It can't be."

Zach snatched the photograph from Angie's hand and stared at the naked body he had once known so well. The masked figure in the photo was undoubtedly Kat.

"Belly button ring, stupid orchid tattoo. It's her Zach. Which means she was getting freaky with Horst."

"Oh God," Zach said. He sat on the fireplace hearth and gripped his stomach. "I feel sick."

"I hate to say I told you so."

"Then don't."

Angie sat beside him and put her hand on his thigh.

"Look, if Kat was getting it on with Daddy Dearest, then maybe the grief from losing him was too much for her. She tried to replace him with you, and when that didn't work she decided to end it all. She killed herself Zach, and leaving the car here was her final act of revenge against the family of the man she always loved."

"No."

"Yep. I bet if we search the vineyard we'll find her all tangled up in the trellis wires…"

"Shut-up, Angie."

"…a reenactment of their kinky love sessions. I wonder if she knew that she was only one in a long line of perverted sluts?"

"Angie!"

Zach exploded. He stood up like a shot, knocking Angie to the floor. Suddenly he wanted to hurt something, someone. He grabbed the fire poker standing closest to him and hurled it across the room with all his might. It hit *The Blood of Christ* painting and sent the offensive thing crashing to the floor. Zach stood there panting like an animal, his head spinning.

Angie knew she had him now. There was nowhere to run except toward her. She pulled herself to her feet and walked to the desk. If they could come together now she would never have to doubt him again. And she had to be sure of his loyalty to her. There was only one thing to do. Zach stood staring at the place where the painting had been, a square area two or three shades lighter then the rest of the soot stained wall. Angie eased herself into the space between her brother and the desk. She stroked his face with her hand. His eyes were stone cold, his nostrils flaring. She killed Kat, he thought. She fucking snapped and killed Kat.

"Our souls are one soul. As soon as you stop fighting that everything will fall into place, Zachary. Everything." Angie slipped a long twig into his hand that she had retrieved from the kindling pile. She turned away from him, kicked off her shoes, and leaned over to place her elbows on the desk. Her heart was doing Pavlovian flip-flops. "We need this, Zach. Horst made sure of that."

For a moment Zach wanted to tear her apart. He wanted to grab her by each leg and rip her in two like a wishbone. He wanted to cut her flesh with the switch tightly griped in his hand. Angie could feel his desire radiating off his skin behind her. It was her desire too. Pain had replaced pleasure for them years ago because pleasure—the visceral kind, between siblings—was taboo. But hadn't the lines had been crossed somewhere, or at the very least blurred beyond recognition? When did it become too much? Angie felt Zach tense behind her and found she couldn't answer her own question. She began to turn so she could see his face.

Zach grabbed her by the neck and pushed her facedown onto the desk.

"You think I'm stuck in the muck with you, Angie, but I'm not. I don't need to beat you, I don't need to fuck you, and I don't need to listen to you. My soul is my own."

He took her arm and bent her wrist back and up toward her shoulder. She whimpered. This wasn't the kind of pain she was expecting.

"Now. What do you know about Kat?"

She didn't answer, wondering how much he dared to tighten his grip. He might as well break her, Angie thought. He might as well kill her. Without him, she was only half a being. She firmly believed that. If he seriously thought she had done anything to Kat, he had failed her.

"Nothing," she whispered.

"Angie, don't lie to me!" Zach's voice began to crack.

She shook free of his grip and flipped over, facing him. They inadvertently fell into a lover's embrace. Their eyes met and they both saw sadness. It was the same look, the same emotion. Maybe they were one.

"Here. Horst would have wanted you to have these." Angie reached over and pulled Horst's notebooks out of the bottom desk drawer where she had left them, the letter from their mother slipped inside their pages. Let him find it for himself.

Zach looked at the notebooks and then back at Angie before he released her from his grip. He shook his head and left the room slowly, quietly, without looking back at her. Zach spent the remainder of the day and into the night meticulously combing the vineyard for signs of Kat. This time his sister was wrong again. No matter how hard Zach looked among the leaves and shadows, he found nothing.

CHAPTER TWELVE 12

12 · AQUA VITAE ·

Horst's notebooks drew Zach in like magnets. They were worn and some of the script was faded in places, with loose scraps of paper that Horst had apparently tucked and stapled in over the years. Each notebook was dedicated to a different wine type, and most read like a laundry list of ingredients and numbers. It was only when Zach began to page through the Merlot notebook that he saw something different. On the second page the word 'emergence' caught his eye and he began to read:

> AN EMERGENT PROPERTY CAN APPEAR WHEN A NUMBER OF SIMPLE ENTITIES OPERATE IN AN ENVIRONMENT, COLLECTIVELY FORMING MORE COMPLEX BEHAVIORS. TRANSUBSTANTIATION? ALCHEMY? IF JOINED CORRECTLY, THE CONTENTS OF THE VAT CHANGE ONE ANOTHER IN A WAY THAT CAN FEEL LIKE MAGIC. WE ARE NOT DEALING WITH SOMETHING AS BASE AS A RECIPE. LIKE ANDERSON SAID, 'AT EACH LEVEL OF COMPLEXITY ENTIRELY NEW PROPERTIES APPEAR. THE WHOLE BECOMES NOT MERELY MORE BUT VERY DIFFERENT FROM THE SUM OF ITS PARTS.' THE AQUA VITAE, THE ESSENCE OF LIFE, NOT CAPTURED OR ABSORBED, BUT RATHER EMERGENT—

Zach poured over the notebook all morning. Anything to escape thoughts of his sister who he could see pacing the widow's walk like a phantom. He sat outside the Lab in the chilly air and read a page or two, read them again, then fell into a long stare at the vineyard while he tried to make sense of his father's musings. He knew the word transubstantiation from his theology class. It was the process by which bread and wine become the body and blood of Christ. It made sense for Horst to have an interest in the romanticism of such a process, and in alchemy too, but emergence? And why were such notes only present in the Merlot notebook? Was Horst simply losing his mind, or was he on to something more?

Then again, maybe the ingredient that made the Merlot so spectacular wasn't an ingredient at all. Maybe it was the energy Horst spent obsessing over it. Maybe the Merlot was nothing more than a reserve batch like Flint had predicted, and Horst himself was its missing link. Emergence and the Law of Attraction are, in a way, two sides of the same coin, Zach thought. They both appear to be magic at first glance, but when broken down…. Zach thumbed open the notebook again to the lines that kept drawing his attention:

> REMEMBER! THE PHYSICAL ESSENCE OF A THING CANNOT BE DESTROYED, ONLY RECREATED, TRANSFORMED. THE ESSENCE OF LOVE AND THE ESSENCE OF WINE CANNOT BE SEPARATED THEY ARE TWO HEARTS BEATING AS ONE, EACH CONSUMED BY THE OTHER, AS THEY PASS FROM SHELL TO SHELL. THERE IS NO DEATH IN THIS LAND, ONLY OLD HORIZONS SEEN ANEW.

Zach read the lines several times, wracking his brain for their meaning. A clear answer seemed to hover somewhere in the back of his mind, if he could only just make the connection between his father's words and the undefined suspicions he was beginning to harbor about Horst's winemaking methods. Flint had called it his "tricks of the trade," so sure that Zach had been privy to this part of his father's lifework. But even with the notebooks, Zach was just as in the dark as he had always been when it came to Horst. After several hours of this Zach came to the only logical conclusion he could think of. He had to get a look inside the vat. No use speculating when he could engage his senses.

He got up to look for Gabriel when his train of thought was interrupted by the all too familiar sight of Sheriff Griffith's patrol car coming around the bend. His heart dropped past his stomach and started on a rollercoaster ride around his large intestines. Not knowing what else to do, he waved like an idiot.

Sheriff Griffith waved back and parked his car on a bias across three potential parking spots. He got out, smoothed his comb-over and readjusted his hat.

"Hi there, Zachary."

"Howdy Sheriff," said Zach. He grimaced inwardly. Did he really just say howdy? "Here on more unofficial business?"

"Sorry, my boy. This time it's official. Miss Slater's been missing for over twenty-four hours. I'm gonna need to have a word with Angelina."

"She's up at the house."

"Looks like you've been busy." Jim gave Zach a once over. His clothes were dirty and sweat stained, and his hands bore long, superficial scratches.

"What?" Zach asked. Thinking the sheriff was alluding

to the notebook he still clutched, he quickly closed the thing and stuck it under his arm.

"You've been working the fields?"

"No."

The boy was acting strange and this time it was the sheriff's duty to read into it. Jim took out his notepad but before he could speak Zach interrupted him.

"I'll um, I'll have Rudy take you up. To the house. I gotta check on the Merlot. It's emerging."

"Okay son. Next time then," Jim said.

Zach nodded and made a speedy exit, forgetting, for the moment, his plan to explore the vat and continued in pursuit of the bigger picture.

Ten minutes later Jim found himself sitting at the large butcher's block table in the Bartlett's kitchen. He had been there before on similar, albeit more easily resolvable grounds. Samantha had come home with a fresh crop of Indian burns that she credited to Angie. He had sat in that very same spot while the girl shed crocodile tears and apologized half-heartedly to his daughter in a way he suspected was a thinly veiled threat of more to come. The father sent her to her room and promised to take care of it. But the behavior didn't stop, though Jim could never prove it. From that point on Samantha refused to name her tormentor, and eventually he was forced to send her to Catholic school.

Jim tried with all his might not to allow the past to influence his detective work, but he couldn't help feeling a tad uneasy around the girl who, now a full grown woman that had just lost both her father and stepmother, sailed gracefully around the kitchen preparing him coffee.

"I wish I could be more of a help, Sheriff, but everything Zach told you is the truth. Tight-abs was here, then she left. Along with everyone else."

"Tight, what?"

"Abs. Our little pet name for her." Angie slid a mug of toxically strong coffee in front of Griffith. "She was a favorite of both my brother and I."

"What do you mean *a* favorite?"

"We both fucked her now and again. But really, that's not saying much. A girl like Kat gets around, if you know what I mean. Have you checked the local roadhouses, strip clubs, brothels, that kind of thing? I bet you could find a whole slew of her admirers, but as far as Zach and I wanting to do her any harm, it was quite the opposite."

Jim recoiled at her candor, though he tried not to show it. Something about being in a room with Angie made him feel mocked and disrespected. But she was talking, and he would play her little game if it meant uncovering vital information. He cleared his throat and pretended to jot a note down.

"How so?"

"Money of course. Kat found a buyer for Lapis. They're offering five million. Why in the world would I go and harm someone who could make me stinking rich?"

"So you kids are planning on selling?" Jim suppressed a smile.

"Well, I want too, but Zachary—he's got it into his head that maybe we should stay and continue the family tradition. With all the excitement around here I haven't had a chance to convince him otherwise, but I will. Give me time." Angie sat down and faced him. "Drink your coffee. Sheriff. It's nice and strong."

"Thank you." Jim took a sip of the bitter sludge and forced a smile.

Angie returned the smile and leaned in over the table, engaging him with all the sincerity of a Stepford wife.

"How's little Samantha doing? You know, I was a

vicious cunt to her in high school. I hope she doesn't hold any grudges. When you see her, please tell her how very sorry I am."

Jim didn't answer her. If she was sorry he was a monkey's uncle. Besides this was no time for small talk. He pulled a small snapshot from his pocket and put it on the table facing Angie. It was the picture he took from Kat Slater's desk at Coldcrest, the one of her and Zach in their eveningwear.

"Remember this?" he asked. "I'm guessing junior prom, right?"

"Actually that was the *senior* prom. I went with Ashton Warren. That night—oh god—Zach and I were crowned King and Queen. It was an anonymous vote and nobody knew how it was gonna turn out so they just had to go with it. The principal was so freaked out. It was hysterical. They wouldn't let us dance together, isn't that dumb? I mean Zach and I dance together all the time. What's the big deal, right? They thought it would come off as incestuous. Hey, did Samantha have a prom at Holy Name of Mary? Oh wait, it's an all girls school, right?"

Jim straightened in his chair.

"They had their prom with the boys at Saint Augustans. But I'd like to talk about Zach if that's okay with you. You say he doesn't want to sell, that Kat was pushing him to?"

"I didn't say that. He doesn't know yet that he wants to sell, but he'll come around. And she wasn't pushing, I'd say it was more of a thrusting."

"They had intercourse? At the wine tasting?"

"In the new kitchen. She was sitting on the counter with her legs wrapped around his hips. He was really letting her have it. But with a girl as loose as that it was probably like throwing a hotdog down a hallway."

Jim fought the imagery and moved on quickly. She

was trying to rattle him. It wouldn't work.

"Then there was a fight?"

"A fight? Hardly. No, Zach was mad at me for getting drunk and interrupting their '*love making*' session. But it wasn't a fight."

"What happened after that?"

"I went to the Lab to say my Rosary but before I could even get started, Miss Slater showed up for a little erotic asphyxiation. I guess one Bartlett simply wasn't enough for her."

"So you had intercourse with her too?"

"No silly, we're women. She strangled me till I orgasmed and lost consciousness. When I came too she was gone. Spoil sport."

Jim cleared his throat and took a large swig of coffee.

"And where was your brother when you *came too*?"

"Zach? I don't know. Here I suppose."

"You suppose?"

"I'm not his keeper."

"You didn't see him at all the rest of the night?"

"No. I was drunk. I spent the night in the vineyard getting in touch with nature."

Jim scribbled a few illegible notes onto his pad, but he pressed down too hard and the tip of his pencil broke.

"Miss Bartlett, I'm going to ask that neither you or your brother leave town until all this is sorted out."

"Until all *what* is sorted out?"

Jim rose from the table slightly disoriented with an overwhelming urge to flee and go straight to confession. The next time they spoke, he promised himself, it would be at the station house.

Angie was disoriented too. Why was he asking so many questions about Zach? She followed him to the back door.

"All what, Sheriff? Zach didn't do anything wrong. He worships that piece of trash. It's disgusting."

Jim turned and faced her. "I'll bet that makes you ten kinds of angry. Doesn't it, Miss Bartlett?"

Angie stood, mouth opened, eyes blank. He almost caught her but she recovered and smiled demurely.

"Give my love to Samantha," she said, waving sweetly before slamming the door behind him.

Later that evening Angie found herself lounging on the floor in the study, tossing darts at giant portrait of Tilda. Because there was no one around—or alive—to stop her, she had drawn a series of circles in lipstick starting with a bull's-eye around Tilda's nose. The circles grew progressively wider in radius as they moved outward, each one worth a designated amount of points. She kept score by carving notches into the polished wood floor with a broken dart, a bottle of Kestrel's Two-Ton Cabernet by her side.

She heard the front door open.

"Zach?" she called.

Gabriel appeared in the doorway.

"Oh." Angie flung a dart in his direction, purposely missing him and hitting the neighboring wall. "It's Captain Tight-lips."

Gabriel removed the dart from the wall and returned it to Angie without comment.

"You seen Zach?" she asked casually.

"He took the truck. I think he went out to search for Miss Slater." Gabriel stepped closer and gazed expressionless at the dart-riddled portrait. "There are two police cars parked outside the gate."

"Great. Thanks." Angie stood up and leaned on one hip. "So um, Gabe, I know we've been over this but if there is anything, anything at all you'd like to tell me about, oh, what the *fuck* is going on here, I'm ready to listen. Because

The Donald and his cronies are suspecting Zach now and if you don't want me ripping this place apart grape by ever loving grape, you will tell me what you know. Comprende?"

Gabriel nodded slowly, still staring at the portrait. Without meeting Angie's gaze he reached into his bag and pulled out a stack of mail fastened with a rubber band. He turned and handed it to her.

"It's over a weeks worth. I must have forgotten to check it." He put the small bundle in her hands and left the room before she could protest.

Angie flipped through the envelopes. Bills, magazines, fliers, leaflets, and finally, something interesting. It was a small handwritten envelope with no return address. She tore it open without hesitating.

> DADDY
>   My little payment is late! Naughty Daddy. Don't make me scratch you! You know what happens if you don't pay your Kitty Kat. Especially if you want to hear me purr. Until then...
>
> XOXO

Angie dropped the rest of the mail in her hands. It went cascading to the floor in a semi-circle around her. She stepped over it and ran out into the hall.

"Gabe! Gabe! You crazy fucker, what did you do to her?" She rushed into the kitchen but he wasn't there and that meant he could be anywhere. She ran up the stairs and through the dark house to Horst's office. She intended to climb up to the widow's walk and scream bloody murder until Gabriel was forced to come back and deal with her head on. But as she crossed Horst and Tilda's bedroom, a room that felt increasingly like an empty viewing room in a funeral home, her pace slowed as if the ground was liquefying. A line of light filtered from the office through the fireplace, illuminating the foot of the bed beside her. Angie stopped in her tracks. A chill shot down her spine. Something didn't make sense.

It wasn't Gabriel. It couldn't have been. Gabriel didn't so much as say boo without Horst's approval. He was a lieutenant, a lackey, and even if he was behind Kat's disappearance, he wasn't acting independently. He had to be following orders. But whose?

The shaft of light from the office flickered slightly and Angie swore she heard the very distinct, though faint, sound of a page being turned. Angie wanted to turn and run but something was pulling her forward. It was Horst. Or the ghost of Horst. She couldn't be sure, and at that moment, she couldn't decide which prospect was more terrifying. She moved forward toward the light in the office only because the thought of leaving and being pursued was unimaginable.

Angelina. She could almost hear him say her name. He would surely punish her for what she did to the portrait, not to mention the countless other punishable things she'd done over the years, all the little sins that he could clearly observe from the omniscience of death. Would Eve hold him back? Would she stop his hand or would she lounge beside Tilda on the bed, unsympathetic, unswayable?

Angie took another step forward. Then another. Maybe if she rushed the room—yes, that would do it. Horst would be waiting for her in the corner directly to her right when she entered. He liked to take them by surprise. He would have made a great magician. He'd step out of the shadows or rise out of the fire like an

✝

unholy Lazarus and either way she would be ready for him. She knew his tricks. Angie took a deep breath, squinted her eyes and ran. She pushed against the door with her body and spun around in the air releasing a scream of anticipation. But the room was empty.

The small door leading to the widow's walk was cracked. She vaguely remembered leaving it open earlier, though she couldn't be sure. A cross breeze caught the pages of an old book lying open on the floor. Angie realized that she, not Horst, was the last person to have been in the room—but only in the physical sense. Horst was all around her, his soul ripped apart in a display that boarded on disgraceful. The room looked like a Mafia looting, or a book burning waiting to happen. She stepped over the carnage and retrieved *The Blood of Christ* from the floor where it had landed *earlier* and returned it to its rightful spot on the wall.

She slumped in Horst's chair. Maybe he wasn't a bad man, maybe he was simply a bad father. Could she stretch her mind to pity him? To see him as an aging winemaker, his work withering in the shadows of progress and youthful exuberance, a kinky old deviant who had to pay women to act out his cliché fantasies—as a victim who was blackmailed by a young temptress to the point of desperation. Could she ever really see him like that, powerless and, well, dead?

No. She didn't think she could, actually. Not because she was too hurt, or too afraid, or even too resentful to get past it. She just couldn't kill the dragon that was her father quite that easily.

Angie's eyes eventually fluttered to the desk. Sitting front and center, the space around it cleared away, was the photograph of Kat that Angie had found with the others. She looked at Kat's naked body hanging from the trellis wire, footless and masked. It hadn't been there like that before, of that Angie was dead sure. Angie picked up the picture and scanned the office around her. She wasn't afraid anymore, only curious.

Angie studied the photograph. It had been left there for a reason. It had to have been. Maybe there was something else to it that she just hadn't seen yet. She studied the picture, looking past the strikingly disturbing figure of Kat, past the vines, deep into the twilight sky over the familiar hills of her childhood. Suddenly, there it was. It almost appeared to be a shadow but once her eyes caught it, it was impossible not to see it clearly.

It was a Kestrel hawk circling high in the air over the hills, leading her mind like a compass to the exact spot where the ritual had taken place. The shape of the hills made it undeniable. She was looking at the north field, the place where Lapis's land boarded Kestrel's. There was an old mew over that hill. It had entranced both Zach and Angie when they were small. The whole family used to picnic in a spot close by, and they would stay all day just to watch the hawks. That's where she was meant to go. That's where she was being led. The picture was a map and Horst was daring her to find him.

CHAPTER THIRTEEN 13

Zach didn't realize he was being followed until he made the final turn towards home in the small hours of the morning. Somewhere in the back of his mind, back behind the exhaustion and the worry, he was disappointed with himself for not noticing the automobile that had been shadowing him for hours. Guys in detective movies always knew when they were being followed and he saw himself as one of them, savvy and cool. You only *look* like James Bond, he reminded himself. He thought of Cassie, the girl back at Bard who had first likened him to the martini sipping, fictional spy. He had wanted to know which Bond of course—a simple enough question he thought. Did she mean Sean Connery or Roger Moore? Pierce Brosnan or Daniel Craig? Alas, she couldn't, or wouldn't, say. Angie had once observed that he had Timothy Dalton's grin. Zach tried to confirm it in the rearview mirror, then scolded himself for accidentally making eye contact with the policeman tailing him.

Zach marveled at his mind's capacity to negotiate his crowded thoughts. Cassie, Bard, Bond, all these things seemed otherworldly now. Like dreams of a former life. It was odd that they already seemed so distant. He'd only been back in Prosser for three days.

The unmarked car behind him joined two others parked outside Lapis' gate. They didn't attempt to follow him in, and he figured that meant they didn't have a search warrant. The land on either side of Lapis Drive was private property, though the road itself was not, which gave the policemen a right to be there. Zach imagined himself bringing them coffee and bagels in the morning, so they knew that he knew that he was being watched, a kind of Tony Soprano move. He wondered what Angie had said to prompt a three-car stakeout. He wondered how long they would stay.

Zach parked the truck and dragged his tired body into the house, up the stairs, and into bed. In the seconds it took for him to fall into a deep, coma-like sleep, his mind played back the disappointing video reel of his sad, one-man search party. He had tried all of his and Kat's old haunts. Prosser's only bar, the hot air balloon shed where they went to make out, a special spot on the river where they liked to lie back and watch for shooting stars. It was stupid, and he knew it, but he couldn't help himself. Something was telling him he knew where Kat was. It was just a feeling though, and the exact location continued to elude him. In his state of sleep deprivation his mind began to play tricks on him. *Go to sleep and we'll tell you where she is*, the voices in his head promised. Reluctantly, he gave in.

Angie heard Zach come in the house. She was lying stone still on her bed, fully clothed, on top of the covers, waiting for first light. She loved the dawn, especially on gray days, and while those were rare in Prosser, she could feel a change in the air that she always credited to a downward barometrical shift.

She wanted to leave earlier, but negotiating the trip in the dark was too dangerous. The north field was on a hillside that got steep in places. She figured it would take her about a half an hour to get there on foot so she left approximately twenty minutes before sunrise, timing it so she would hit the rough terrain just as the sun appeared to guide her the rest of the way.

Angie pulled on her old pea coat, fished out a pair of galoshes from the annals of her closet, and slipped out the French doors onto the balcony. It was her old escape route. During her teenage years she was constantly being caught shimmying down the columns past curfew, so much so that Horst eventually placed sentinels around the grounds to watch for her. It worked until she realized that when she really needed to sneak out all she had to do was wait until everyone was in bed, go down stairs and walk right out the front door. Not an option now thanks to the police detail at the front gate. She wondered what idiot thing Zach had said to provoke a fucking three-car stake out. She wondered how long they planned on staying.

The balcony was also a direct path to Zach's room. She could see him in there now, curled up in his bed, his clothes in a pile on the floor. She thought of waking him but decided against it. If she did find something up there on the north field, she wanted the option of taking it to her grave.

She swung a limber leg over the rail and spun her body around with practiced ease. She locked her legs around the column and lowered her body past the balcony floor. Once secure, she released her grip and inched down like a gorilla descending from a palm tree. After a few minutes her feet hit the ground with an ungraceful thump. Been a while, she thought, shaking her head. She looked around her. The air was cold, the vineyard still and silent save for the occasional birdcall, and it was dark. The only light was a small amber pool emanating from the front porch, and that wouldn't help her for very long.

Angie started down the path that led to the migrant shacks. It was the quickest and easiest way to the north field. She knew the terrain well, even without the help of the flashlight she had stuck in her pocket. As she passed the migrant housing she saw that Gabriel's light was on. She could hear the soft sounds of the Spanish language station broadcasting the morning news, and she wondered again if it could have been Gabriel who set her on this path to begin with. Logically she knew it must have been, but there was another force pulling her forward into the night. It was something that had nothing to do with Gabriel, Lapis, or any of the surrounding civilization that had sprung up in the years since her parents took over the vineyard. The force was more primal than that, as though the vines themselves were calling to reveal to her their true and hidden purpose.

The pueblo ended at the head of a small path, the one that would take her up into the untamed hills. In the years since her mother died, Horst had slowly reduced the amount of tended and harvested land. His staff had shrunk from fifty to ten, and the edges of the property where the plots were less accessible, had been left to grow wild. The north edge of Lapis had been virtually ignored for years.

Angie hugged the path in the dark. Once the migrant shacks were safely behind her she flipped on her flashlight, cutting a beam of light through the oppressive blackness. Whoever said it is always darkest before dawn was right, she thought. She continued on the narrow dirt path, only the sound of her breath and her own footsteps to keep her company. For fifteen minutes she pressed forward on a slight incline that took her further and further north into the hills. The path finally ended headlong into the meticulously tailored vines of Kestrel's fields, forcing Angie to cut further east into the wild overgrowth where her final destination lay.

The sky began to brighten right on schedule. As Angie pressed deeper into the thicket, she felt like the prince in

Sleeping Beauty cutting his way through a forest of thorns. How hopeless, she thought. What in the world did she expect to find up here anyway? She thought about going back to the house, but she felt foolish turning around. No matter which direction she went she had to watch her footing. Overripe grapes littered the ground making it slippery and dangerous. Vines grabbed at her legs and got tangled in her hair, and she could picture herself twisting an ankle and being stuck up there to rot forever. Maybe that was Gabriel's plan all along. If she were out of the picture, he could have Zach all to himself. In time, Zach would become just like Horst only easier to manipulate. Every Igor needs his mad scientist, and without her there to convince him otherwise, Angie was suddenly sure that Zach would fall for all Gabriel's false flattery and step into the roomy shoes of his precious Enóloga.

Angie stopped, out of breath. The vines were so thick she could almost sit down and be supported on all sides, as though enthroned by grapes. She took the picture of Kat out of her pocket. The hill in question was still further north. She could see it from where she stood, but the angle was wrong. Her mouth was dry and she would have kicked herself for not bringing a bottle of water if could she locate her feet. After a moment's rest, and for reasons she couldn't explain even to herself, Angie pressed on. A Kestrel hawk out for his morning flight circled gracefully overhead. Must be an omen, she thought with a shudder.

Twenty yards and five minutes later Angie was able to see a change in the terrain ahead. Ten yards and two minutes later she could tell it was a clearing, but it wasn't until she finally stepped from the thicket that the whole picture fell into place. The photograph lined up perfectly with what she saw before her: the row of vines, the hill, even the morning hawk. Even though she had half-expected to find Kat in the same spot as the picture depicted, Angie wasn't entirely surprised to find an empty space at the center of the vines. Marking the spot on the ground was a shallow hole that seemed innocent enough until it was put into its macabre context.

He buried their feet there. Angie caught her breath and slowly approached the guilty spot. Lengths of wire hung in twisted clumps off the trellis, some of it old and rusting, some of it newly cut. She let the tips of her fingers caress the cold metal and wondered what it must have felt like stretched tightly over bare skin. Following her fingers to the coiled edges of the vine she noticed, tangled within it, a mask of leather and feathers. In a flash she understood: Horst had used it to blind them. And though she fought the image, she couldn't help but wonder which part of the process aroused her father the most.

But why here? Because it was secluded? So were more easily accessible parts of the vineyard, that was for sure. No, there was something else about this spot. Horst and Eve had dragged them here as kids, she remembered that. As a matter of fact, she wouldn't have been surprised if most of the family pictures from Horst's desk had been shot here. What was so special about this place?

Was this...? Angie struggled to corral a memory. There had been a stone, a blue stone. Lapis lazuli, the philosopher's stone, the most sought after object in alchemy. Horst had one, not literally of course, but.... The memory came hurling at her like a boomerang that had been tossed into an abyss years before and was only now returning. She caught it like a pro.

Angie pushed past the row of vines. A few feet behind them, the ground took a sharp upward turn. She dug through a layer of foliage and pushed aside some loose dirt. On the night that Horst and Eve took over official ownership of the vineyard they made love among the vines. *Naming their new child Lapis, the ancient philosopher's stone, the holy grail of the alchemist.* How many times had Horst told them that story when they were young? *And what is winemaking without the powers of transmutation?* Again, she could almost see him, questioning her with his cool glare.

There it was.

He had carved it with his own hands, for that's what he was born to do. The Thannhausers were quarry men, sculptors and church builders, descendents from a long line of heretic alchemists. The slab of deep blue lapis lazuli was engraved with the words, *In Vino Veritas.*

"In wine there is truth," Angie whispered.

She gripped the stone with both hands and pulled with all her strength. She could feel that one of the sides was loose so she concentrated her effort there. With another yank she fell backwards, not only with the stone in her arms, but also with the trap door it was attached to.

"Holy shit." Her voice echoed back to her from the depths of what she'd uncovered. It was a tunnel that seemed to lead straight into the hill. Angie took out her flashlight and shone it into the darkness. From what she could tell the tunnel sloped downward and ended at a door. Though Angie wasn't the type who spooked easily, the creeping gray dawn did little to sooth her anxiety. Part of her wanted to run back to the house and wake Zach before doing what she found herself doing, slowly making her way down the tunnel towards the door.

The dank smell of earth consumed her senses. Every third or fourth step she took she pause to check over her shoulder. For some reason she couldn't help but anticipate the slam of the outer hatch, trapping her forever in darkness. The tunnel itself wasn't very long, but from inside looking out at the grey

sky it felt like miles. She had to stoop as she reached the end, her claustrophobia mounting. Though she had a sense of ominous foreboding, at that moment she preferred the unknown contents behind the door to her present situation. With a deep breath, she hastily pulled the handle open.

More darkness. A step down. Angie's flashlight played over the contents of the hidden bunker, among them a row of several single-bulb lights overhead. She turned towards the wall and searched for a switch. She found it and switched the lights on, illuminating a curiously predictable sight. It was a wine cellar. She let out a nervous laugh that sounded odd even to her ears. Of course it was a wine cellar. What else would it be? Casks lined the dirt walls each enshrined in their own catacomb-like enclave. The place felt old, and not old as in years, but old as in eons. She switched off her flashlight and took another nervous glance backwards, towards freedom. Deciding everything was as it should be, at least for the time being, she allowed herself a look around.

There was nothing remarkable about the cellar. The only thing strange about it that Angie could see was the barrels themselves. They were stored in cubbies dug deep into the walls of the cellar. Above each one was a plaque bearing the name and date of the vintage, and below, on small dirt altars, were makeshift shrines sporting a combination of dead flowers, candles, and small statues of various saints and deities. Angie examined each one. Chateau Genevieve, Chateau Antionette, Chateau Maria, Chateau Giselle. They're all named after women, she realized.

Angie heard a distant cracking sound and quickly turned on her heel. She peered outside just in time to catch the shadow of a figure making its hurried way into the tangled vines. Her heart sank. Suddenly she wanted nothing more then to get the hell out of there.

She switched off the light and slammed the cellar door, making her way out of the tunnel as fast as humanly possible. Her breath was heavy and she was shaking but she tried to be quiet so she could listen. Whoever had been following her either knew a shortcut out of the field or was somewhere lying in wait. Angie decided not to hang around and find out. She closed the outer hatch with the rock and quickly rearranged the leaves and dirt to hide it as best she could. Then, without once looking back, she made her way towards home.

CHAPTER FOURTEEN 14

14 · SOLVE ·

Zach was climbing the walls. He hadn't seen Angie all morning and the presence of the police had shifted his mood from inquiring, to suspicious, to downright accusatory. They were watching Lapis like a bunch of blue and white guard dogs and to make matters worse, Flint and his marketing man Jacques had decided to come by for a little impromptu visit. Zach had hoped to get a look inside the Merlot vat, odd paranoid scenarios playing out in his head thanks to the subtext written all over Horst's notebook, but Gabriel was acting strangely. Zach saw Flint's truck coming up the drive as he and Gabriel were in the middle of an argument over whether or not it was a bad idea to open the vat until it was ready. Gabriel insisted it was, with a stubbornness that put Zach into a muted rage.

"It's not ready," was all Gabriel would say, as if this was somehow a good enough reason to disobey Zach's orders.

"The cake needs to be punched down though, doesn't it?" Zach followed his father's assistant around the Lab like a desperate puppy, trying in vain to reason with him. "You're just going to let it sit? It will compromise the wine."

"The men already mixed it this morning, Zachary. You can do it tomorrow."

Gabriel went infuriatingly about his business without looking Zach in the eye. To top it off he had placed Rudy and Gerardo on the catwalk like a pair of watchful gargoyles to keep Zach out of the Merlot vat.

"This is my vineyard now, Gabriel. I'm the Enóloga. You have to do what I say."

Though he seemed momentarily impressed by Zach's assertiveness, Gabriel refused to budge.

"It's not ready."

Zach felt like he was losing all control. A feeling followed shortly thereafter by the realization that he had never had any. Gabriel, Angie, the cops, they were all playing him like a cheap fiddle and he'd had enough of it.

"This is insane. Open it. Now!" Zach ordered, his shout falling on the ears of his guests, Flint and Jacques, who stood silhouetted in the sliding door of the Lab.

"Bad time?" Flint asked.

Zach spun around as though ready to attack, but the sight of the two men forced him to gain his composure and act as if his whole world wasn't descending into chaos.

"No," Zach exhaled, "It's just...."

Flint waved it off with an aura of calm that Zach immediately resented.

"Those cop cars would rattle anyone."

"Yeah."

"I had no idea it was as bad as all that. Shouldn't they be out looking for Kat instead of harassing you guys?"

"You'd think." Zach couldn't suppress his sarcasm, nor did he try.

Flint gave him a sympathetic grin and a pat on the back that made Zach cringe just a little.

"Well, that's why we wanted to come by, to show our support. I had a word with Griffith. Told him that we were backing you and Angie one hundred percent."

Zach softened a little. That was nice of him, if it was true.

"You remember Jacques, right?" Flint asked.

"It's been awhile," Jacques said, extending his hand, "But I'm a big fan. Your father left quite a legacy here."

✞

"Thanks," Zach said, shaking Jacques' hand. He vaguely remembered meeting the man who many credited as the genius behind Kestrel's rapidly growing publicity. At one point even Horst had reportedly made him an offer to switch ranks, an offer that Jacques politely refused with no hard feelings on either side as far as Zach knew.

There was a pause where both Jacques and Flint seemed to be waiting for Zach to say more. Jacques rolled backwards on his heels and exchanged a look with Flint before peering over at the closely guarded vat in front of them. Zach shook his head and pretended not to notice. He was in no mood for forced pleasantries.

"Is that the only reason you stopped by, Flint?"

Flint smiled and raised his brow in an expression that seemed to say, *you caught me.*

"I guess curiosity killed the cat, right?"

There was an awkward silence as the three of them tried to ignore Flint's conversational misstep.

"Well, Let's taste some wine." Flint suggested heartily.

Zach gave Gabriel a nod and Gabriel brought out the glasses.

"Quite a secure operation you have going on here, Zach. You think the batch is that good?" Flint joked trying to lighten the mood. Rudy and Gerardo stood grim faced, neither had budged from their assigned posts.

"I know it is, Flint. And I heard you coming up the drive, so…."

Flint laughed a little too hard, relieved to hear Zach shifting into a playfully competitive tone of voice.

"You wanna do the honors?" Zach asked Flint provoking a slight advance from Gabriel who quickly corrected himself when Zach shot him a look.

"Is that okay?" Flint asked, picking up on the bizarre exchange.

"It's fine," Zach said, shifting his weight to block Gabriel's view.

As Flint captured the wine, Jacques leaned over towards Zach.

"So Zach, you're thinking of taking over the family business permanently?"

"I don't think I have a choice until those cops decide to let me leave town."

"And your lovely sister?"

"What about her?"

"She's a bit of a winemaker herself, isn't she?"

"No. Well, I guess, but she's more of a wine drinker actually."

Flint handed the glasses around with just the slightest bit of haste. The mere mention of Angie made most who knew her uncomfortable, even the unflappable Flint. And even Zach found it hard to force all thoughts of her from his head. She was just too much. Over the past few days he wasn't really sure if he knew his sister anymore. Or maybe the reverse was true, that he knew her too well and the series of events unfolding around them were, in fact, their destiny. Zach stood there, and for the first time, felt sure of something that didn't have to do with wine. Angie, damn her, had been right all along.

"Cheers," Flint said. He raised his glass and studied the color before closing his eyes to drink. Jacques followed suit and Zach, with his eyes wide open, also let the garnet liquor hit his lips.

Oh God. He knew. All the pieces suddenly jumped up and fit into place like a class full of excited demon children who suddenly knew the answer to a question posed by the Devil himself. *Nightmares are real and reality is but a convincing fraud,* they screamed in unison.

As the other two men savored the moment, Zach looked over at Gabriel. A current passed through them, from one man to the other, from old to young, a current of silent affirmation. Gabriel raised his chin and took a sharp breath in through his nose. Zach checked his own expression. His mouth was hanging open and he closed it, locking his jaw in a line of acceptance. In that split second he aged countless years. Some part of his destiny was nearing its tragic completion. Time seemed to stand still as Flint and Jacques, the winemaker and the connoisseur, dislodged themselves slowly from the feeling. In them, Zach was witnessing the final stage of the wine's emergence, the final complex system imposing its will. *Aqua vitae.* The essence of life itself.

"Sublime," Jacques whispered in a tone that sounded almost post-coital.

"Zach, it seems your men are guarding a treasure after all. It is an extraordinary Merlot," Flint said.

"It's more than extraordinary. It's my father's masterpiece." Zach bowed his head as though reciting Horst's final eulogy. The men honored the moment with silent reverence.

Flint put down his glass.

"It needs to be barreled now! Today. Tomorrow at the latest. Get your men on it. And if you don't mind, we would like to stay. We could help, couldn't we Jacques?"

"Absolutely. It would be a pleasure."

Gabriel was about to step in but Zach didn't need him to, not this time.

"No, thank you, gentlemen, but the barreling of this particular wine is to be a family affair. I trust you understand. As soon as I locate my sister…."

"Zach, Zach!"

The men turned around. Angie came barreling into the room at a mad pace. Her hair was wild, her face flushed, and she was covered up to her knees in mud. Zach's heart did a flip-flop but he tried to remain calm on the outside.

"Speak of the devil," Jacques said.

Angie came to an exhausted halt in front of them.

"What are they doing here?" she asked.

"Hello, Angie," Flint offered.

"Hi," she said without glancing at him. "Zach, I need to speak with you. In private."

Zach's eyes met hers.

"All right. Our guests were just leaving."

Zach and Angie took the golf cart as far as they could up to the north field, though at the edge of the cultivated land they were forced to make the remainder of the trek on foot. Angie led the way. They didn't speak much, neither one of them revealing the secrets they'd discovered, as though saying them out loud would some how make them real. There would be time for that later. In the meanwhile, they took in the trip with long bouts of solemn and mutually respectful silence. Every so often one of them made a comment about their childhood memories of the north field. In a way, they were bidding farewell to that very childhood and entering the secret world of their parents. Somehow they both understood that it was a world from which it would be impossible to return.

They arrived at the clearing that Zach remembered from the photographs. He sighed. So it was here that his star-crossed lover had met Horst, undressing for him, playing out his sick fantasies. Zach wanted to feel something. He knew he should. But it was the way it had always been with him. He had to be told what to feel, guided by the feeling half of his person, the skinny-legged kewpie doll standing to his left in bright green galoshes. He stared at the ritual spot. It looked so vicious in the daylight, a piece of the puzzle he could barely comprehend. He wanted to say something, to do something but he was as stuck as a baby in a well. He felt his sister's hand in his.

"Come on."

Angie guided him past the row of vines. She swept back the leaves, revealing the Lapis stone, and pulled back the hatch.

"My God, I remember this now," Zach said. "Horst brought us here once. But that was so long ago…."

"I know. Come on."

Zach followed her into the tunnel and to the door. She opened it and flipped on the switch. The lights flickered on with an audible clink. Nothing had been visibly disturbed that Angie could see. She gestured at the horseshoe-shaped row of casks that wrapped around the cellar.

"They're all named after women, the women in the pictures. There were twelve pictures, and look, there are eleven casks."

Zach made his way around the barrel shrines, examining each one with curiosity.

"Who are they?"

"Migrant workers, mostly. Remember Maria? Look." Angie led Zach to the cask labeled *Chateau Maria.* "Maria-Grazia was her full name. I remember because Grazia means Grace, and she was anything but graceful. I used to pull her hair, remember? She was in her teens when she left. And Giselle was that Jamaican girl who came up here the summer Flint was around. God, I hated her. I thought Flint liked her and I was so jealous I could hardly see straight. But it looks like she had her eyes elsewhere after all."

Zach only half listened to Angie. He had turned his attention to the opposite wall where an unoccupied thirteenth cubbyhole lay in wait.

"So what's that for?"

"I don't know. Are you listening to me? These are *shrines* for godsake. He wasn't just fucking them, he was worshiping them damnit."

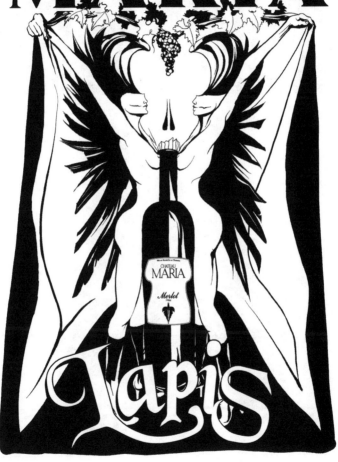

"Horst?" Zach turned to her with a skeptical look.

"Yeah, I know. I don't see it either. But what else is this sick shit about? Besides, Maria and Giselle left years ago."

Zach had turned his attention away from Angie and bent down to study some of the items on the altar closest to him.

"They left?" he asked, without looking back at her. "Or they disappeared?"

"What?"

"Why do we prune?" Zach asked suddenly. He lifted a pair of rusted sheers from the altar in front of him and stood facing the wall.

"Is that a rhetorical question?" Angie walked over and leaned her head softly against his shoulder.

"We prune for the sake of the vine. We cut off extraneous shoots and canes, we thin and crop the clusters, we remove any sign of disease so the vine can grow strong and produce better fruit. Don't you see? Don't you know where this is leading us?"

Angie didn't answer. She didn't know. All she could do was hold tightly to her brother's arm and hope against hope that he wasn't cracking up. She looked up at him. He was staring at the cask above the altar where he had picked up the pruning sheers, the first in the row. She followed his gaze to the name carved into the plaque above it. Her grip tightened on his arm as she stared at it with him. For the first time she understood what they were seeing. *Chateau Genevieve.* Like the patron saint of King Arthur's queen, it was a name with many diminutives. There was Ginny, Jenny, Genie, and, of course, the one staring them in the face. The most humble and sweet diminutive of them all, comprised simply of its final three letters: e, v, and e.

CHATEAU GENEVIEVE

Mis en bouteille au Château
CHATEAU
GENEVIEVE
Merlot
1984

TAPIS VIN

PROSSER

CHAPTER FIFTEEN

15

It seemed Angie had been right about the weather. On the way back from the north field the rain came down in sheets, making conversation nearly impossible, especially with the focus Zach had dedicated to driving the golf cart over the slippery dirt road toward the main house.

"I still don't understand," Angie shouted over the engine, holding onto the edge of her seat so she didn't slip off the side at each bend in the road. "If they all disappeared, wouldn't someone have noticed by now?"

"You said it yourself," Zach said as he bent closer to the windshield and increased his speed. "They're mostly migrant workers. Except—"

"Except Mom."

"Yeah." Zach came to a halt in front of the Lab and closed his eyes for a moment. When he opened them he shook the steering wheel once with both hands, drawing in a deep breath at the same time. "And Kat," he added.

"Kat?" Angie looked at him incredulously. "You can't be serious. First off, Horst is *dead*, Zach, in case you missed that vital piece of information. And second of all, the bitch was blackmailing him. Yes, really. I found the letter that proves it. She's probably halfway to Fiji as we speak."

"Maybe."

"Maybe?"

"Or maybe that's exactly *why* she had to disappear. Someone else could have made that happen, anyone who knew. But just forget all that for the moment.

There's something else to all this. I kept trying to put my finger on it, and I just think…I don't know. Didn't you notice in there? All the wines? They were all Merlots. It's something in the Merlots, Angie, I'm almost positive. You've got to trust me on this one."

"The Merlots? Zach this is hardly the time to play Master Winemaker. Can't you see…?" Angie stopped short when she realized that Zach wasn't listening or waiting for her as he strode towards the steel doors of the Lab. She hurried to catch up.

When they opened the door they found the Lab lit with candles. Once the twins stepped inside Gabriel closed the door behind them and locked it, nodding at them as if he had known all along that they would arrive just when they did.

"What the hell?" Angie said, turning to glare at Gabriel, but no one answered. Zach took her arm and guided her silently toward the Merlot vat where Rudy and Gerardo were already busy siphoning off the wine into barrels, the spillage from the bottom hatch marking the floor like blood stains. Beside them a thick plastic tarp was laid out on the floor, framed by an eerie layer of CO_2 mist.

In the relative darkness of the Lab it was clear that Angie had gone pale. She was shivering and wet, practically shaking from exhaustion. My Angel, Zach thought, taking her hand.

"All that matters is us, okay?" he whispered.

She nodded and leaned in close to him. She had never felt less sure of herself as she did watching Rudy and Gerardo finish the slow and arduous task of filling the last few barrels. When they were done, Gerardo climbed the steps to the catwalk—thirteen, just like the Medieval gallows. The men knew what to do. Gerardo entered the tank, and after a few moments a pair of arms were slipped out the bottom hatch. Rudy grabbed them firmly and tugged, pulling a purple

and bloated corpse out from the depths of the vat.

For a moment, Zach wasn't sure how he'd react, but when he saw it he felt relieved. This thing wasn't even human. Everything he'd known and loved about Kat had been transferred safely to the barrels lining the wall. All that was left was a crushed grape, an empty vessel lacking in purpose. It was just a shell, and he could not mourn it.

The men carried the body down and laid her on the tarp. Her blonde hair had been dyed a dark red and was matted with pomace, the seeds and skins of the grapes left behind. As Zach tried to think of something appropriate to say, Angie lifted her head from Zach's chest and glanced down at the grizzly sight.

"That's not Kat," she whispered.

It took Zach a second to realize that she wasn't speaking metaphorically.

"What?"

"Where's her tattoo? Zach, that's not Kat."

The twins looked at Gabriel. With a gloved hand and barely an expression, he knelt beside the corpse and pulled back the hair covering her face.

Angie was right. It wasn't Kat. The body piled limp on the tarp belonged instead to their stepmother, Tilda Bartlett.

16 · SILVER ·

"What do you do with the bodies?" Zach asked as Gabriel and the men wrapped Tilda in the plastic tarp. His voice sounded distant to his own ears, as though he were swimming underwater. He had expected to feel sadness, relief, even anger, and now there was this, this appearance of Tilda, the one face he had never expected to see again. If he were acting rationally he would be overwhelmed with confusion, but again there was nothing. Just a cold recognition that this was his responsibility now. A body to be disposed of, barrels of wine to inspect, and ultimately, bottle. The mechanism of Lapis continuing to grind its wheels, slowly but surely. He could either choose to move in turn, or be crushed by them.

"That is none of your concern." Gabriel said. For the first time he peered at Zach with a look of open curiosity. "Do you understand?"

"I think I do."

Zach heard the lock click and the steel doors slide open. He turned just in time to witness Angie running in the twilight towards the main house. He started to go after her, but stopped himself. He looked back at Gabriel instead. "Tell me what needs to be done and I'll do it," he said.

Gabriel smiled and shook his head. "No, Enóloga. There is nothing at the moment. This is our work. Go and find your sister now. It is more important that you both understand." He walked over to Zach and placed his hand firmly on Zach's shoulder. "Your father would be proud. You should know that too."

Zach began to speak but was interrupted by a shout from outside the Lab.

"Enóloga! The policemen!"

Zach and Gabriel looked at each other, sharing the same current of understanding that they had earlier, before Gabriel slipped out the back of the Lab with Gerardo and Rudy in tow. Without a backwards glance, Zach went to meet the sheriff at the front door.

"Zach, please forgive me the hour, but we need to talk," Sheriff Griffith said as he got out of the patrol car and walked over to greet Zach at the doorway.

"Sheriff," Zach said. He was about to protest but Griffith cut him off.

"May I come in?"

"If you're asking I'm assuming that you still don't have a search warrant and in light of that little fact, I'm afraid, once again, I am going to have to ask you to leave. This is turning into harassment."

"No, Zachary, you don't understand. We're not accusing you. It's Miss Slater. We found her name on a flight list headed to the Caymen Islands. She must have hopped a redeye to Seattle and from there, well, we're looking. Believe me, we're prepared to do everything we can to find her."

"Well, that's good, isn't it?"

"Yes, please forgive the interruption. But there's more. We found out the extent of Miss Slater's involvement with your father. I'm afraid it's a little delicate, but he was making monthly payments into her account. We aren't yet clear why, but we do know that she had full access to the Prosser Development Fund and cleaned it out dry as a bone. The morning she showed up missing, the bank records report two and a half million dollars transferred from the fund to some kind of locked, overseas, ah, doohickey."

Zach paused. "Wait. Let me get this straight. Kat

disappeared? I mean, like really and truly disappeared?"

The sheriff shifted uneasily on one foot. He wasn't exactly sure where the fool Bartlett was going with this.

"Well yes, son. I thought we were all clear on that fact."

Zach laughed abruptly, and covered his mouth just as quickly. "No, no, you don't understand," he said, shaking his head. He was aware that he was still grinning from ear to ear, but he couldn't help himself. "You're saying that Kat *disappeared*, poof, gone. With everyone's money. To a tropical island somewhere."

"Uh, yes. I believe that's the gist of it. As I understand it the amount she took in from your father was negligible, but if you're worried about prosecuting, we'll be doing all we can—"

Zach couldn't hold back any longer. He doubled over with laughter that echoed off the high ceilings of the Lab as though a crowd of amused onlookers had gathered around them. He wiped the tears from his eyes, but the expression on Sheriff Griffith's face only made him laugh harder.

"I'm sorry Sheriff," Zach gasped between bouts of laughter, "but we won't be prosecuting. I do appreciate all your time and interest though. We all do." Zach wiped his eyes again, still chuckling, and slapped the sheriff on the back good naturedly. "And happy hunting. If you do catch up with her, please send her best wishes from the Bartletts. With love, of course."

Sheriff Griffith nodded, excusing himself as quickly as he could with a tip of his hat. On the way to his patrol car he could still hear Zach's laughter behind him. Must be the grief, Jim thought. With all that boy's been through it's no wonder he'd end up as odd as his parents, not to mention that twin of his. Jim sighed. At least that was the last he'd be seeing of the Bartlett family for a long time to come. Hell, the way he saw it, if he never saw either one of them again it would still be a day too soon.

CHAPTER SEVENTEEN

17

17·WORLD·

Zach wandered through the main house calling Angie's name until he finally found her sitting cross-legged on his bed, the last place he had thought to look. Horst's notebooks were strewn around her, and there were dark smudges under her eyes where her mascara had run without her bothering to wipe it away. Zach leaned in the doorway with his hands in his pockets and studied her for a minute before speaking.

"Hey there."

"Hey yourself," she said without looking up at him. She held a letter in her hand as if she was in the process of memorizing it.

"The Donald was just here," Zach said, grinning. "He had some news about Kat. Wanna hear it?"

"Not really."

"Oh, c'mon, Ange. Not even the part where she embezzled a shitload of money and ran off to sip Mai Tais until the Feds catch up with her?"

"No and bully for her."

"Seriously? That's it?" Zach stepped over a few of the notebooks to sit on the floor at the foot of his bed and tugged gently at her foot. "Wanna tell me what's up then?"

"What's up? '*What's up?*'" Angie choked, looking over at him. Her eyes flashed and she had definitely been crying, something even Zach had only seen her do a handful of times in their life together. "I'll tell you 'what's up,'" she continued, balling the bottom half of the letter she held in one fist and shaking it at him. "Did you even read this? Did you even fucking bother?"

"Angie, wait, get a grip. I don't even know what you're talking about—"

Angie laughed dryly. "Of course you don't, Zach, of course you don't. Ding-dong, the witch—I mean Baroness—is dead. How'd she end up in the vat, now, in Prosser? Who knows? Who cares? You're too damn worried about your precious Kat anyway, *and* your precious Horst, not to mention your precious fucking wine. How could you spare a moment to think about anything, much less your very own mother? That's right, your mother. Forgot about her, huh? She *is* dead after all. And so long ago too. So who cares who killed her, right? Just water under the bridge for you I guess."

"What the hell are you talking about?"

"This letter, Zach, the one you didn't bother to read. Oh wait, I'm sorry. Here. Let me do the honors." Angie held the letter up to the light and began to read in a loud voice. " '*You may be afraid, but please know that I am not. Can you see? It is inescapable, this destiny. Even when I am gone I will still be with you.*' "

Angie stopped reading and threw the crumpled letter at him, rising from the bed to pace the room like a caged animal. "Do you get it now? She wasn't ever sick. She was leaving him. She didn't want to, but she had to. And he couldn't stand it. He killed her rather than let her go."

Angie stood still in the center of the room, her breath coming out in hard gasps. That was it, there were no tears left. She just wanted to curl in a ball on the floor until time passed and none of this was real anymore.

Zach picked Eve's letter off the sheets where it had landed, flattening the creases as best he could. He read the letter quietly, scanning it again to be sure before he looked up at his sister with wide eyes.

"'The physical essence of a thing cannot be destroyed, only transformed,'" he said. He jumped to his feet and grabbed Angie's arms with excitement. "Go get your flashlight. We're still missing something here, and I think I know exactly where to find it."

Before he even flicked on the light switch in the wine cellar, Zach knew something was different there. It was in the atmosphere, as though a physical charge had settled over the ground where they stood, vibrating with energy. He knew Angie could feel it too by the way her grip tightened on his arm the moment before their eyes adjusted to the light.

"Zach," she breathed.

Zach looked around the room. Even though it felt changed, everything looked much the same as it had before. The barrels were still in their places, along with their shrines and the plaques that gleamed in the dim underground light. Then Zach saw where Angie was pointing, at the empty thirteenth cubbyhole. The ground around it looked freshly swept, and there was a new plaque installed in the wall above it. The twins crept forward together to read the inscription. *2008, Chateau Tilda.*

"I still don't understand," Angie said, frustrated. "Tilda was with Horst, right? When the plane went down? There wasn't supposed to have been any bodies, and yet here she is. Gabriel can take care of the disposals all he wants, but there's no way he's capable of pulling off a magic trick like this."

"So maybe it wasn't Gabriel at all," said Zach, turning away from the empty cubbyhole toward the opposite side of the room. "At least not in the way we're thinking." He bent down again at Eve's shrine, only this time the rusted sheers he'd held the last time were gone. In their place was a bottle so dark it looked black, even in the light. *Chateau Genevieve.*

Propped in front of the bottle was a black and white photograph of their mother's face, smiling. She seemed to be looking at Zach like she knew and understood all that he was feeling, all his questions and worries. Zach turned the photograph over to reveal her familiar writing:

> *Memory made physical, begets love, and the circle continues to turn without end. Any essence that is true only grows larger than its parts, encompassing everything in its path. Pass our gift on to the children when they are ready to understand. Let them join us, if they choose.*

Zach handed the photograph to Angie and cradled the bottle in one hand while she read the note.

"It was in both their letters, you know," he said finally. "The whole bit: physical essences, destruction and resurrection. You can't have one without the other, they both understood that."

Zach set the bottle of wine between them, and stood to take his sister's hands in his own, the shape of each finger perfectly matched to clutch the other's.

"Thing is," Zach continued, "I think they've been waiting for us to understand the same thing."

Angie stared at him as though she were hypnotized by his words. She nodded her head slightly and closed her eyes. Zach moved his hands to her wrists, then her waist, resting his forehead lightly against hers. He closed his eyes as well.

"It was a sacrifice, Angel, what she did," Zach whispered. "It was the only way their love could survive anything, even time. Maybe even especially time."

"And now we are being invited to do the same thing," Angie whispered back.

"Yes, Angel. Yes, I think we are," Zach said. He gathered the bottle of wine from the floor and took his sister's hand, leading them back through the tunnel, out into the endless night in front of them.

DAY 1:
RESTING AT HOME
WITHIN AGED OAK BARRELS,
THE RESULT OF MY ART
NOW BEGINS THE LONG,
DARK JOURNEY TOWARD
MATURITY!

· AMALGAMATION ·

From the widow's walk the Bartlett twins surveyed the vineyards. The rain had stopped and the sky was beginning to morph, clouds receding to make way for another violent Prosser sunset. They watched as day battled with impending night, throwing at it every color in its arsenal, refusing to go down without a fight. What lay before them, creeping silently in the stillness of dusk, was a living legacy, arbitrary yet malleable, a guardian of secrets, the land that held them with deeper roots than they had ever realized. In the end, Lapis was a place they could never put on the auctioneer's block without also placing their own heads beside it. They were tied to the land and its trespasses in the same way their parents had been—eternally.

There was only one thing left to do.

Zach eased the cork out of *Chateau Genevieve*, and set the bottle on the card table to breathe. The twins sat in the two lawn chairs opposite each other without speaking while Zach poured the wine and swirled it in the glass. Without even raising it to his nose he could sense its depth. Angie just looked at hers.

"I don't know if I can drink this. It's strange, you know."

"I suppose," Zach studied the color. A deep black hue hid a garnet heart that he could almost hear beating.

Zach raised his glass to the sky, gesturing for her to do the same. The wine sparkled proudly setting a perfect example for the grapes growing below.

"The bar doesn't get any higher then this!" Zach

shouted out across the fields. Angie threw back her head and laughed, as Zach turned towards her again.

"To Eve?" Zach asked.

"To Eve," Angie replied, taking the glass in her hand.

The wine touched her mouth, her tongue, and in that moment Angie was falling—through time, years, layers of memory like silk veils passing over her skin. She felt the back of her mother's hand caress the length of her cheek, a pair of lips soft on her forehead. Zach had warned her it would be like this. The essence of life, a circle coming to completion. Angie drew in a sharp breath and in that instant she knew the fragrance of sunlight, and understood, finally, what everyone had been trying to tell her for so long. There is no death, she thought.

"Still ready to chuck it all and head back to the city?" Zach asked, resting one hand casually across the arm of her chair.

Angie paused to catch her breath and swirled the wine in her glass, watching it catch the early evening light of the rising full moon.

"Oh, I don't know," she said, stretching out her legs and propping them up on the ledge in front of them. "I'm starting to wonder how *Chateau Tilda* will turn out. Besides," she continued, raising her glass to his again, "who knows. I've always had a taste for Cabernets."

It was Zach's turn to join in Angie's laughter as the twins shared one last toast to the future rushing in at them over the fields. They both knew it was a dark and mysterious future, one with no death, only another page to turn.

Dedicated to
Genevieve Mileto
a.k.a.
Nonnie

The Merlot Murder Mysteries is a series of mysteries set in vineyards all around the world. The production of each title is a collaborative effort and is specifically designed to showcase each of the artists contributing to the book. We strive for artistry in all aspects: concept development, writing, editing, original artwork & book design, and finally creative publicity and marketing.

Our production process is much like that of wine: a loving sowing of inspiration, careful cultivation, severe pruning, and artistic finessing. But the experience doesn't stop there. The art continues through you, the reader. Like all great books, you become part of the art! The concept exceeds the confines of the book, planting roots that grow in the minds and hearts of its readers. Loved books are either passed from hand to hand or by word of mouth to become a source of social connectivity—that last vital ingredient that establishes a true art form.

We encourage you to experience all aspects of this book. Put your feet up, read the story, and linger over the artwork. Sip an exceptional glass of Kestrel's wine and then become part of the art by sharing it with your friends.

TIGRESS PUBLISHING
PRESENTS
THE MERLOT MURDER MYSTERIES TEAM

KRISTEN MORRIS:
Founder & Ceo of Tigress Publishing,
Marketing Guru, and Event Wizard.

STEVE MONTIGLIO:
Innovative Artist, Fugitive Musician,
and Defender of Truth.

D. MICHAEL TOMKINS:
Award Winning Author,
Bad-ass Attorney,
and Original Concept Engine

FOR THE SAKE OF THE VINE
FEATURING:

ADRIA LANG:
Author, Siren Screenwriter,
and Burlesque Diva.

AMELIA BOLDAJI:
English Language Samurai,
Publicist Extraordinaire, and Writer.

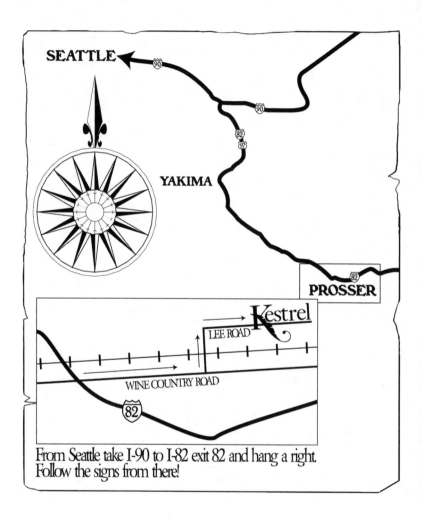

From Seattle take I-90 to I-82 exit 82 and hang a right.
Follow the signs from there!

SPECIAL THANKS TO

Kestrel

VINTNERS

our partners in crime
when it comes to this book, that is.

(We don't need to say it but we will: All bodies in vats are completely ficticious!)

Kestrel Vintners, a real winery located in Prosser Washington, is not only an award winning winery, they are also a collective of talented, brave, and forward-thinking marketing geniuses. Kestrel's creative team includes Owners John & Helen Walker, General Manager Michael Birdlebough, Marketing Director, Jacques (J. J.) Compeau, Master Winemaker Flint Nelson and a dedicated staff. As a team who understands well the power of collaboration, they have now partnered with Tigress Publishing to create *For the Sake of the Vine*.

Kestrel Vintners is committed to producing excellent wines at reasonable prices. Most of the 33,000 cases now produced annually are reds. These wines are lovingly crafted to suit wine lovers with pallets for dark, rich reds, whether they are looking for a Cabernet Sauvignon, Merlot, Sangiovese, Syrah or Kestrel's collectible Lady in Red blend. About 15 % of Kestrel's production is also in white wine, from their Chardonnay and Viognier, to their Pure Platinum, a collectible white blend.

The key to Kestrel Vintners' success is the Kestrel View Estate Vineyard, which is home to some of the oldest Chardonnay, Merlot, and Cabernet vines in Washington State. Its central Washington location provides two additional hours of sunlight daily compared to California's prime growing region.

To order the award winning wines represented in this book, please go to **www.kestrelwines.com** where you can also join their wine club to receive invitations to special events, and news from the winery.

Kestrel Vintners
2890 Lee Road . Prosser, Washington . 99250

CHATEAU GENEVIEVE

CHATEAU
GENEVIEVE

Merlot
1984

PROSSER

LAPIS VIN